CW00871005

FLOOD

TOM WATTS

SPRINGBOARD

1995

Published by **Yorkshire Art Circus**
School Lane, Glass Houghton, Castleford
West Yorkshire, WF10 4QH
Telephone: (01977) 550401

Events and characters in this novel are entirely imaginary. Any
similarity to real events and persons is coincidental.

© Yorkshire Art Circus, 1995
© Text, Tom Watts
Edited by Graham Mort
© Cover illustration by Mark Taylor
Cover design by Jane Crumack

Typeset by Yorkshire Art Circus
Printed by FM Reprographics, Roberttown

ISBN 1 898311 12 9

Classification: Fiction

Springboard is the fiction imprint of Yorkshire Art Circus. We work
to increase access to writing and publishing and to develop new
models of practice for arts in the community.
For details of the full programme of Yorkshire Art Circus workshops
and our current booklist, please write to the address above.

Yorkshire Art Circus is a registered charity (number 1007443)

Acknowledgements:
Pat Baddeley, Ian Daley, Fiona Edwards, Olive Fowler, Reini
Schühle and special thanks to the members of the Yorkshire Art
Circus reading group.

We would like to thank the following organisations for support
towards this book:

Yorkshire & Humberside
A R T S

West Yorkshire Grants

City of Wakefield
Metropolitan
District Council
Leisure Services

For Harvey

Chapter One

Thirty years was a long time. But the churchyard hadn't changed much. Fuller, of course, more overgrown. The view from the low sandstone wall that marked its southern boundary was the same, more or less. A few hedges had gone from the other side of the valley; the fields were bigger. But that was progress, according to the fools who made short-term profits from such notions.

Bob was not a believer in progress. He had seen too many men become slaves to it - bosses and workers alike; seen them mesmerised by its glittering lure and hooked, like trout in a bouncing stream. Bob was a believer in ghosts. It was the past that had the real power. That was why he had come back.

He'd had no idea the new bypass would take him so close to the river - he'd merely glanced at the map and decided it was his quickest way north to the next contract. As he chugged along in the Landrover, with the big caravan behind, he'd had plenty of time to pick out the woods and farms and field tracks he'd once known so well: Wild Man and Willow Farm and the winding path through the riverside pastures he had walked that day with Sally Bell. He could see the pale stone of the priory reflecting the sun and the dark outline of St Margaret's church on the skyline, with the rumpled field to the east that was the Roman Camp. Then the sunlight flashed on the river and he looked away.

As he drove the ghosts came surging back like a spring flood. As soon as he felt them stirring in his blood he knew, this time, he would have to do something - he didn't know what - but something to try to still them.

Was it just morbid curiosity? Was he possessed? A bit of both. But there was also a need. Not to atone - that was impossible. Not to make amends. Not even to exorcise the demons. But to resolve a certain confusion, to replay the old film, if he could bear it, with greater clarity: how did it happen; how could it have happened?

He hadn't been so close to the town for ten years. But, then, the wounds had still been too tender for him to think of stopping.

He had driven through the villages, skirting the town, his hands clammy on the steering wheel. But the new bypass was an unexpected twist of fate inviting, at last, some sort of confrontation.

Part of those ghosts had never left. They came to him now with renewed power, not just from his memory, but from the landscape. It was as if, all those years ago, he and the others had left some shadowy substance of themselves in those fields and woods, some flickering energy that still flitted among the trees.

Bob pulled into a lay-by, but left the engine running. He stared in the mirror at the threadbare remnants of his once rich ginger hair. No. No-one would recognise him now. Besides, it was early, not quite six o'clock. He could spare an hour and be gone again before the town was properly awake.

Taking the first left turn off the bypass he followed the new road through the hazy summer sunlight into the valley towards the town that straddled the river. That town. His town. Burial place of the undead.

It was ironic, he thought, that he should be arriving after all these years on a summer morning, with the mist thinning over the fields in the sunrise. He had a brief sense of *déjà vu*: it had been just such a morning when he had run, desperate and confused, through the riverside fields for the last time... But, then, life is nothing if not ironic.

As he descended he had a feeling of increasing pressure, as if he was going down in a diving bell. Don't worry. Don't react - just keep going... For the thousandth time he cursed his curious sensitivity to place and mood and glanced quickly behind him, half expecting Old Florrie to be perched among the ropes and chainsaws. As the neat new semis began, the suburban illusion of an ordered world, he realised he was sweating.

A few milkmen were about. He ignored them. One or two paper boys on their bikes. The muscles in his cheeks twitched. He saw an image of Mouth, bumping along back street cobbles on his old Raleigh tourer.

He nosed through the quiet streets towards the centre of the town. Approaching the river bridge he glanced about quickly,

5

trying to assess the changes that had taken place in his absence, struggling to fight clear of the undertow of guilt which swirled towards him from the familiar sights that still remained. He wanted to shut his eyes as he arrived on the deserted bridge, to blot out the sight of that river. But he kept them open and there it was: dirty brown from the peat that washed down from the hills, as weed-choked as ever, dark, deep and ominous.

The dye works to the north of the river had gone; in its place was a housing development. The feed mill was luxury flats. The brewery had disappeared completely - a Tescos supermarket stood on the site. And Reeds - Christ, where was it? No sign of the great blank facade that had dominated the lower end of the town. He wound the window down quickly and sniffed the air like a questing animal. Not a whiff of that unforgettable sulphurous stench. Nothing! A long flight of wide steps led up from the road. Then a smart glass doorway... Jesus - a sports centre! Bob laughed aloud in surprise. That was the second irony of the day. In that street he had known so well only the Black Swan on the corner had survived.

He drove slowly along the main street noting the names above the shops. About half of them were ones he didn't know. He resisted the temptation to drive around the market square to look for Nelson's and old Ralph's and followed the parking signs instead into a wide side street. To his surprise he found himself facing the river again. Then he realised where he was: the place they used to call the Swamp, between the senior school and the river, had been turned into a car park, with a new reinforced floodbank topped with a few flowering shrubs. There wasn't a boggy hollow or willow sapling in sight, not a single tuft of the mats of couch grass where he had gone after morning lessons with Sally Bell. He drove on to new tarmac through the precise spot where the old school had stood. He was sure. Not one dismal grimy brick of the place remained. Now, Bob thought, that's definitely progress!

Parking between two immense transcontinental containers Bob felt as anonymous as the car park. No-one drove further than London or Glasgow in 1959... His Landrover had Dyfed registration plates and he had bought his caravan from a gypsy fellow up in the Borders. He was almost invisible: a working bloke in a brown boiler suit, on his way for a piss and a morning paper.

St Margaret's church on the hill was five minutes' walk from the Swamp. Or he thought it was. But in 1959 he had never walked anywhere, preferring to use his lightweight racing bike, that orange coloured Carlton, even to go to the chippy round the corner... That Carlton, he mused as he walked, suppose they must have looked for it. But they would never have found it. If they had, they would surely have assumed that he had died.

It took Bob ten minutes to walk to the church. The heavy wrought iron gate had a broken bottom hinge and had gouged a deep groove in the path. He shoved it open with his workboot and stepped through, tense all at once, sensing that the dead were expecting him. The sight of the soot-blackened bulk of the church tower did nothing to reassure him. Jesus, what a filthy place this was.

He tried to work out which were the newest graves, wondering how many of his family had died since he went away. His parents, perhaps? If they were still alive they would be in their early seventies... And where was his sister these days? All at once he wanted to make contact, to end the lonely fugitive years, wanted laughter, warmth, welcome... But no. The gulf was too vast. Unbridgeable. For ever.

He paced up and down the overgrown paths, glancing at the dates on the headstones: 1872...1921...1947...1960... Nothing after 1960. The rest must be buried in new ground someplace. But his grandmother might be here. Old Florrie was that ancient she could have died in '59 or '60. He peered at the gravestones: Hardisty - Peel - Temple - Simpson. No Ellises. Old Florrie was still alive in 1960, then. Perhaps she was too old to die. Perhaps she just faded away into her teacup or into the strange shapes she fancied she saw in her fire.

He reached the last row of graves. Beyond was a new brick wall and a line of petrol pumps. Used to be Nicholson's field. Nicko must have sold it off - always said he'd get rid of it soon as it was left to him. He continued his survey: Thompson - hell, that was Thomo's dad. Only forty-nine... Nugent. Hardisty again. And the overgrown small one in the corner. He bent to decipher it. Funny, he thought. There's no day on this one. Only May 1959, above the name Ricky. Could have been a pet dog.

He stepped back quickly. A chill swept through him like an icy breath from a grave. His blood began drumming in his ears. Oh, Christ! Oh, Christ, of course - it was him!

He leaned on the churchyard wall in the strengthening sun, staring out over the riverside pastures. His first inclination after seeing the grave had been to flee. But he had done that for the last thirty years and he had no will left for flight. He hadn't much fear now either. Fear had simply faded, becoming fainter and fainter over the years, thinning almost to nothing like his hair. He still had the horror though. That was as fresh as the night's slugtracks on an overgrown gravestone.

Thirty years on the run but he hadn't escaped. How could you escape? His guilt had brought him back like an iron filing to a magnet. This town and the riverside fields were full of it. He could feel it all around him like a living presence, watching him, willing him to weep, to go mad, to confess. Old Florrie's sensitivity. Her blessing and her curse.

The place was full of his sadness too; full of his anger and hurt and that terrible unexpected isolation. He relived again the pain of those betrayals - the pain that had made it almost impossible to be close to anyone since...

Thankfully there had been times when the past had been silent, when he had been too busy or too tired for memories to upset him. But they were always there, biding their time, waiting. At the sight of a torn overcoat, or a rifle, or a flooded river, he would have to turn away, catching himself fingering the hairline scar that ran across his left cheek.

Gradually Bob coaxed his attention into the landscape. The council estate had grown - only one field left and then it would reach the priory. They should call that field Sally Bell's Close - she had given him such a time down there... He saw her again, as he had so often before, hitching up her aunt's tight skirt as he

8

helped her over the fence, and he felt the tug of yearning in his stomach. Sally Bell: the first and, he had to admit it, the best... He shut his eyes and felt the moisture beneath the lids.

He had known, after only a couple of weeks, that his flight had undone him. But it was too late by then. It was him because he had gone. Obvious. Open and shut. But what else could he have done? He was considered by the police to be a troublemaker. He had been seen in the riverside fields. And then there was Brock... Enough.

The fact that he hadn't been found was because he had run fast and far. He had left the town and the county; left his name, his nickname. He had chosen a new name, just like that, and no-one had ever questioned it. Ronald Patterson had been consigned to the slim family photograph album and a file in the police station.

And Young Red had been abandoned on the riverbank, like a beached wreck, as Robert Patten had made off with his life. But, Bob reflected, Young Red had also stolen Robert Patten's.

It was time to bring the two of them together - if he could. To reconnect them, face to face. Then, maybe, they would treat each other with a little more sympathy. That was the best he could hope for. There was no way he could ever bury Young Red. And he couldn't turn the clock back and stop being Robert Patten either.

Bob's eyes wandered again over the valley. The dense willows and alders of Wild Man, the bumpy pasture of the Roman Camp, the pale ruins of the priory... How little had changed here in thirty years... The river was low now, though. Not like that day in 1959 - the day of the freak spring flood. The flood had been the reason for their going. Without that flood he would have had such a different kind of life. Married now with grown up kids. A cottage in one of the villages, or a new semi on the edge of town... A foreman at Reeds, following on from his dad - till steel production became history... Then probably some kind of driving job to see him through to retirement. But he couldn't imagine such an alien world. It seemed more removed than the moon. That hadn't been what he'd wanted.

Staying or leaving, either way, he felt his life had been damned. By others. By himself. But then, Bob thought, glancing at the small grave in the corner, there are so few lucky ones.

CHAPTER TWO

Young Red's morning paper round took him past St Margaret's church, which stood on the highest point in the town. He was nearly through his round when the cool air stimulated his need to pee. Relieving himself behind a tall Victorian headstone he gazed east over the rooftops of the town towards the river. He had stared at the view from the churchyard almost every morning for the last eighteen months and he felt he knew it as well as he knew his own reflection.

This morning he was dazzled by the sunlight flashing from what looked like a plain of glass, just beyond the town where the river had been the day before. For a moment his sleepy brain struggled to understand the nature of the sudden change. Then, because it was Saturday, he let out a huge yell, remounted his bike at a run like a rider in Wells Fargo, and hurtled from the churchyard.

A short while later he cycled impatiently in circles at the end of his street, waiting for Mouth to finish his round so he could break the glorious news. At the end of the longest five minutes of the week a lanky figure appeared under a black mat of uncombed hair, bumping over the cobbles on a heavy Raleigh tourer.

"Hey, Mouth, it's flooded!" Young Red bawled at the approaching figure. Mouth drew level and stopped with a brief squeal of new brake pads.

"You what?"

Mouth, sullen and surly, twisted his rubber mask of a face into a scowl. He sat so still on his bike all his energy seemed to gather into his eyes, which appeared to Young Red to be so dark no light would ever penetrate them. The scowl and the eyes sent out a single message to the world: danger - keep off.

But Young Red was the one privileged being on the planet who could ignore the signal and get away with it. He was chief of the half-dozen select male friends who could call Len Dykes by his nickname and not get thumped for undue temerity.

"The river, for Chrissake! You can see it from the churchyard. It's flooded right past Wild Man! Must be miles across!"

Mouth's scowl slid into hiding and was replaced by an ugly grin. "Shit! Let's see!"

The church clock was striking eight as Young Red and Mouth freewheeled along the paths between the gravestones. They stopped at the low sandstone wall which marked the southern boundary of the churchyard and stared out over the rooftops towards the river. Mouth's grotesque grin appeared again as he peered with screwed up eyes at the dazzling transformation.

"Christ! Whole valley's flooded! Must have been the thunder storm in the hills last night. My dad told me he drove back through it from Skinner's scrapyard. Jesus, it must have rained." His voice was husky with awe as he turned to Young Red then back again quickly to the view. "Never seen it as wide as that. Water's gone past Wild Man!"

Young Red shielded his eyes from the sun, concentrating on the landmarks he had come to know over the years. "It's gone as far as Willer Farm. That line of poplars runs down from the fold yard. Never seen them under water afore."

Mouth turned away from the view. His scowl was back in place. "Bet it's all gone by tomorrer. Up and down that fast. If we want to see it at its best we'll have to go today. Better get Brock and Raggy."

Young Red looked troubled. He shook his head.

"If we take Raggy we'll have to look after him. Ain't it best to leave him? He could be a problem."

Mouth spat at a gravestone.

"Raggy's useful. Anyhow they've done a lot with him at the deaf school. Taught him to lip-read and that. So you can talk to him when he's watching you."

Young Red was still doubtful. "But he ain't that bright. You never know if he's going to do something daft."

Mouth gestured in impatience at the gravestones.

"You look after him, then, Red, if it bothers you. Tell them we're off to Wild Man. Be at the Roman Camp at half nine, okay? I'm going for my breakfast."

12

Young Red coloured under his fiery curls. "What about my breakfast?"

Mouth's features twisted readily into a sneer. He pushed his wild hair back from his eyes - a simple action, but somehow it seemed threatening. "You live nearer than me. Tell them half nine. And don't forget the rifles - and ammo."

"Bossy sod!"

But Mouth gave him his mocking grin, turned and cycled away, leaving his friend in futile irritation among the dead.

The Roman Camp was a bumpy field which occupied the remaining higher ground beyond the church at the eastern limit of the town. Below the fenced off area of the camp the land sloped gently into the flooded valley, which spread away into distant woods and copses. A group of figures leaned on a gate in the first flooded field below, surveying in silence the wilderness of trees and water. After a while Mouth spoke, still staring into the brilliant distance. "Hey, Raggy, you ugly bugger, you ain't got a gun so you'll have to go first. Get him a stick, Red."

Raggy was oblivious of his three companions. He had wandered away from the gate into the shallow water and stood there, like a marooned scarecrow, in his tattered fawn duffle-coat and patched trousers, staring in fascination at the shining flood. Young Red cut a four foot length of blackthorn from the hedge with his clasp-knife and splashed towards the motionless figure. He had to poke Raggy in the back with the stick to attract his attention.

"You're the Scout." Young Red watched Raggy to make sure he was lip-reading his words. "You've got to tell us of danger. Deep water and roots and stuff."

He couldn't manage any more and turned away in revulsion at the sight of the old chickenpox scars on Raggy's face. Why hadn't someone stopped him picking his spots? Christ and deaf too. That's bad.

"Okay, Red. I'll be Scout."

Young Red winced at the dry croak of Raggy's voice. Over the years Raggy had suffered from so many illnesses Young Red had long ago lost count. His voice seemed to have been baked in some kind of a fire.

"If it's animal we'll shoot it. If it's vegetable or mineral we'll give it a new name." George Brockless, plump and freckled, smiled with self-satisfaction, because he was supposed to be so much brainier than the others - and the town's best batsman under sixteen.

"This water's Lake Brockless and I'm claiming it for England."

"You're a sodding vegetable!" Mouth scowled at the smiling freckles.

"And I'm giving you a new name. It's Porky Brockle-arse, ain't it, Red? 'Cos he eats polony sandwiches!"

Brock's smile was undiminished - he was used to Mouth's taunts about polony.

"You've got it wrong there, Mouth. Vegetables don't eat meat!" His smile widened; he'd scored an easy boundary.

"Don't you ever listen to *Twenty Questions*? I listen to it with my dad. It's better than TV. My dad says you learn more from the radio."

Mouth spat with contempt into the shallow water. "Your dad can't afford a bloody telly! My dad's bought two already. And given one to me!"

"He pinched them from Ozzie Barnett's workshop! He's a bloody thief!"

Mouth aimed a savage blow at the freckles, but found Young Red's strong hand on his arm.

"Pack it in, you two, or I'm off back! You're worse than Ma Preston and her flaming Evangelists for causing trouble!" Young Red knew that Brock got some kind of weird kick out of antagonising Mouth, and it always ended up in a fight, with Mouth thrashing the hell out of him and Brock bleeding and blubbering. Mouth's rhyming couplets would start soon - a bad omen for the outcome of the day.

"Anyway..." Young Red stated with finality, "this is Lake Red and I'm claiming it for myself!"

"But it ain't red, Red."

"It will be in a bloody minute!"

14

Young Red scooped up a handful of water and flung it at the grinning freckles. As he did so he caught sight of Raggy, splashing about twenty yards away, oblivious of their shouting. Their scout had already set off on his adventure, prodding his blackthorn stick into the slowly swirling water at each careful step. Young Red looked at the small shabby figure and thought it hard to believe he was the same age as the rest of them. He seemed more like twelve, rather than just fifteen. He'd been stopped at twelve by his illnesses. He could hear okay once, too. And he wasn't so ugly before he was ill. Came of being poor. Everything went wrong for you when you were poor. Big Red had said so often and, whatever Young Red felt about his father, it was obvious, in this case, he was right.

"Okay - now listen." Mouth was giving his orders. "Keep your guns in your coats till we get out of sight of the houses. Hey, Raggy, you maggot-eaten cheese! Turn him round, Red, so's he can see me... Raggy - we're off to Wild Man. Aim for the field gates and watch out for ditches. Okay?"

They waded slowly through the flooded fields in single file, following Raggy, until they had three fields between themselves and the last buildings of the town. Mouth held up his hand. "Okay - that's far enough."

He glanced rapidly around, like an escaped prisoner, his eyes running along the lines of the field hedges, looking for anyone who might spoil their day. Major Upsall, the shooting tenant, had often given fruitless chase before. Mouth wrinkled his nose, as though at an unpleasant smell.

"No sign of Upshot Bagley." He cleared his throat and spat. "Guess he'd rather drown himself in the pub."

Mouth unzipped his windcheater and revealed the prewar Webley Mark Two, with its detachable barrel, ingeniously taped between the seams. Young Red withdrew his Airsporter and Brock slid his father's old German Original into the light.

"You got enough slugs? Right. Don't shoot at nothing till we've all seen it, okay? And that means you, too, Brockle-arse!" Brock smiled benignly at Mouth's sneering scowl. "Keep to the hedgesides - not too close in case there's a ditch."

"Topped my wellies already." Brock complained as they waded through the shallow water. "Never been down here when it's been this deep."

Young Red glanced down. Brock's trousers were wet below the knees. "Too short in the leg. Why don't you get a longer pair?"

"My dad won't get me any more. Says I have to buy my own wellies when I start in his gang at the station."

Too skint, more like, Young Red thought. Platelayers don't get much. Any spare cash Brock's dad had probably went on cricket whites... At the mention of work Young Red felt suddenly gloomy and oppressed. That was the world of Big Red and his union talk. The world of Reeds and his own future. Young Red hated the future. When he got there he would enter a world that seemed to make folks so sad. It was a world that made his father angry with everyone, especially with him. Without the future, Young Red thought, life would just go on as it always had: hunting down the river fields and being chased by Upshot Bagley. It would go on being fun...

"Who the hell'd give you a job?" Mouth mocked the smiling freckles. "You're still a wetneck. You haven't even been with Belly yet."

Brock's fair complexion flushed and he flinched from Mouth's scornful stare. "You've only been with her once!"

"So? It's more than you've ever done, you pissing wetneck! Red and me spent a whole afternoon with her in the priory last September - didn't we, Red?"

"Sure did, pardner!" Young Red grinned like a newly elected president. "Best tits this side of Jayne Mansfield!"

Brock smiled smugly. "Some have brains and some have pricks - and I know which makes the most dough! One day I'll be a station master. And you'll still be selling scrap with your dad!"

Mouth's eyes seemed to grow darker than ever. His face twisted into a mocking sneer. Young Red's heart sank as he heard the first of the day's rhyming couplets.

"Brock's a clever dick..." Mouth's chant continued, soft and menacing, "Brock's a clever dick, but he hasn't got a prick. Brock's only got a brain, so he'll never get a dame. Brock's - "

"Coot at ten o'clock!"

Raggy had stopped abruptly and Young Red, who was walking backwards, watching Brock's masochistic agony and wondering why it gave him so much pleasure, stepped heavily into him. He recoiled as if he had touched a corpse.

"Christ, Raggy! What you do that for?"

Raggy nodded ahead and to his left. Young Red tried to avoid looking at his face. Raggy wouldn't get a dame either, he thought. Not without plastic surgery. And how would the poorest family in the town ever afford that? His thoughts were cut off by Mouth's fierce whisper in his ear.

"Four of them. Field corner. See? We'll stalk them along the hedgeside. Watch out for the ditch. Hey, Raggy - you go first."

They crossed the flooded field and circled around the coot, following the hawthorn hedge until they were less than fifty yards from their prey, close enough to kill with the powerful underlever air-rifles. The birds were swimming in circles, clucking with hard metallic voices.

"They've seen us." Mouth whispered, his face taut with excitement. "Aim for the one by itself on the right. Go for the head above the shield. Everyone. I'll count one-two-three-fire. Okay?"

"Okay."

The coot was hit in the head and set up a violent commotion. Blood darkened its bright white shield as it thrashed its wings, treading water in a futile attempt to fly and calling dementedly. Its three companions flew low and fast, skimming the water's surface, as Young Red followed their flight with his empty rifle.

Mouth's rubber features creased with disapproval. "Stuff it, Red. It ain't a shotgun."

"Might be one day."

Mouth's attention switched to their scout. "Hey, Raggy - go fetch it, boy!"

Raggy had abandoned all caution. He had dropped his blackthorn stick in the water and was running wildly through the shallow flood in pursuit of the wounded bird. The coot was taking a little while to die and had started to gyrate on the water in a prolonged nerve-spasm. Raggy caught it up and grabbed its twitching legs. He hoisted the bird aloft in triumph and was instantly showered with water, blood and excrement. The three hunters roared with delight.

"Do it again, Raggy!"

"Hold it up and do it again!"

But Raggy only grinned, unable to lip-read in his excitement. He waded back to them with the feebly flapping bird. Mouth took it from him and casually wrung its neck, tossing the limp rag of a body high into a hawthorn.

"Something for Upshot Bagley to scratch his stupid head about."

"Might think he's going mad, seeing a coot in the top of a tree, instead of on water, and blow his head off in a fit." Brock giggled at the image he had conjured up.

"I'll blow your bleeding head off, Brockle-arse, you simple sod!" Mouth paused, eyeing Raggy with a mock-crazy stare. "What's nature anyway, Rag-arse, but a breeding machine - like women? The more holes you blow in it the more bloody kids pours out!" He turned away and spat. "You should know, you poor bugger, your stupid mam's had eight of you!"

But, Young Red knew, it wasn't Raggy's mother who angered Mouth so much. It was his own, and for reasons other than breeding. He looked away, avoiding Mouth's eyes, not wanting to humiliate his friend by revealing that he understood his pain.

Raggy grinned up at Mouth as if he was a hero, unable to lip-read his bizarre conversation. Young Red eyed Raggy with increasing distaste. "For Chrissake wash your blasted face!"

Raggy stared intently at the limp bird hanging in the tree.

"Dead." He croaked, smiling and staring at the bird, as if recognising something for the first time. "Dead and gone."

He waved his arms in clumsy imitation of bird-flight, flapping and turning in an ungainly circle. His eyes rolled, showing the whites. The others looked at him in mute surprise, sensing the strangeness of the moment.

"I think Raggy's getting soft in the head." Brock whispered to Young Red as they plodded in single file again along the hedgeside. He smiled in self-admiration. "It's probably 'cos of all his illnesses. He ain't getting enough oxygen to his brain."

"It's 'cos of his being poor." Young Red, without thinking, spoke with his father's voice. "When you're as poor as that you're bound to be a bit weird. Doing without so much can make you strange."

He realised he was playing Big Red again and made a determined effort to add something of his own. He frowned with concentration and spoke more slowly. "He won't have eaten anything since yesterday. Mebbe even the day afore. Stopping eating can make you funny in the head. Like a yogi." He grinned. He was pleased with that last bit. That bit was Young Red at his best.

"What the hell do you two know?" Mouth rounded on them suddenly with unexpected force. "He's weird 'cos he's Raggy. He's old Ma Bottoms-up's kid! And that's all there is to it!"

"That don't make sense, Mouth." Brock protested, but Young Red gave him a warning look and he lapsed reluctantly into silence.

As they walked Young Red pictured again Raggy's shabby flapping figure. There was something about it that disturbed and intrigued him. Raggy had unnerved Mouth, too, but he would never admit it. He would have to talk to Old Florrie about it some day. She would know. To Old Florrie strangeness was normal.

They shot a couple of water voles that had been flooded out of their burrows in a field drain. The voles had nowhere to hide and dived when they saw the hunters. They stood back from the drain and waited, rifles at their shoulders. When the voles came up for air they shot them. The dead voles bobbed up to the surface and drifted away on the imperceptible current towards the central flow of the river. As they drifted their speed increased, until the current took them and swirled them out of sight.

At Brock's insistence they retreated to a little grassy knoll that stuck up about a foot above the flood so he could empty the water from his wellingtons. While Brock struggled with his sodden socks Mouth and Young Red lounged in the grass and rested. Raggy noticed Brock's labours and took his wellingtons off too. But he had no socks to wring out.

"Christ - poor sod ain't got no socks!" Mouth stared at Raggy, wrinkling his nose.

Young Red saw that Raggy's black wellingtons were speckled and streaked with green paint. "Been painting your house, Raggy?"

But Raggy only grinned and shoved his bare feet back in his boots. Mouth laughed. "Pinched them off a painter fella, most like. While he were busy up his ladder!"

They lapsed into silence, staring at the flood. Young Red frowned.

"It's dry on the top of this hill. The water's never reached it." Mouth pointed with the barrel of his rifle. "You can see where the floodline comes. Where the water's flattened the grass. That means it's been higher."

"Means it's going down. Hey, Raggy, borrow your stick a minute." Young Red stood up and planted Raggy's blackthorn wand at the edge of the water.

"Now we can time its fall."

He looked at his watch, the old Ingersoll he had bought from the pawnbroker's with some of his savings from his paper round. "Fifteen minutes."

"Give us a cig, then, Red, it'll help me wait better." Mouth never carried cigarettes. His father searched his pockets almost every night and always took anything he could use, including money.

Young Red produced a packet of Du Maurier and he and Mouth smoked for some minutes in silence while Brock twirled his socks around his head like helicopter blades in an attempt to dry them out. Raggy stared like a sadhu into the shimmering distance.

"Belly said we could go down the priory with her again if we got her some cigs." Mouth spat at the blackthorn stick but missed.

Young Red looked at his watch. "Ten minutes gone." He glanced at the stick. "Going down, ain't it? When she say that?"

"Yesterday. After assembly. Said we could go anytime we liked." Mouth cleared his throat and spat again, hitting the stick. His slightly contemptuous expression never changed. "She said now it was May and warmer."

Young Red looked at his watch. "You going?"

"Might. You?"

"Might. Eleven minutes gone. How many cigs she want?"

"Twenty." Mouth spat. "Twenty each if you come."

Young Red looked at his watch. "Might. Have to see."

"Let me know, then, and I'll tell her."

"Sure."

Young Red looked at his watch. No-one spoke for half a minute. "Twelve minutes gone."

Mouth shifted on his elbow, still watching the stick. "You hear that, Brockle-arse? Me and Red going to get laid with Belly. You coming?"

Brock stopped twirling his socks. He blushed, staring at his naked feet. "Dunno. I might."

"You going to get her some cigs?"

Brock squirmed. "I... I dunno." He rubbed his feet. "I... I might."

"Then what you going to do when you've give her the cigs and she's laid on her back on the grass and pulled up her skirt and said come on, George, do it to me?"

Brock started struggling with his socks, blushing, tugging at the damp unyielding material. Mouth removed his eyes from the blackthorn stick and turned them on Brock. His face was a mask of scornful amusement.

"What, Brockle-arse? What you going to do to her? Come on, Brockle-arse - like women, don't you? Like to get laid with Belly? Like to feel her fingers touching your little cock-a-doodle-doo?"

He laughed harshly and chanted, "Belly lay in the grass with little George Brockless, and Brock started to blush when he saw she were frockless; come on, George, aren't I worth stuffing? But he looked in his pants and couldn't find nothing!"

Brock was pulling desperately at his wellingtons, trying to haul them on over his twisted socks. His bottom lip trembled

21

and he seemed on the brink of rage or tears. Mouth stood up and turned towards him, but found Young Red was on his feet too, blocking his advance.

"Fifteen minutes is up." Young Red spoke woodenly. "Water's gone down two inches."

Mouth plucked the stick out of the soft earth without looking at it. "Flood'll be down by tonight. Like I said. Here." He passed the stick to Young Red. "Wake him up and let's get going."

Young Red had to poke Raggy with the stick to bring him back from his meditation. They set off again in single file. For the next half hour Mouth ignored Brock completely, looking past him as if he was invisible. Peculiar bastard, thought Young Red. Don't know why I hang around with him. Tormenting the poor sod just because he doesn't like girls...

But he would go anywhere with Mouth at any time. Because Mouth always led them into danger.

CHAPTER THREE

By midday they had shot a moorhen and another water vole and were all wet through to the thighs and jubilant. They had waded for miles through the flooded fields and had reached the wood known as Wild Man. Lying their air-rifles carefully across the lowest branches of a young oak they perched on the woodside fence, drumming their heels against the middle rail and staring solemnly at the gleaming flood like a group of castaways.

"Have you ever asked Old Shack how this spot got called Wild Man?" Brock had recovered from his humiliation. "He's only bloke left who's likely to know, ain't he?"

"Don't know Old Shack that well. But I can ask my gran."

"You think Old Florrie'll know? She that old?"

"My gran's nearly a hundred. There's nothing she don't know." Young Red was surprised by the vehemence with which he praised his grandmother's omniscience.

"I know she reads tea leaves and stuff. But what's she see in them?"

"She sees things in the future. And sometimes from the past. And she sees stuff in the fire too."

"You ever seen her do it?"

It was unusual for Brock to ask so many questions, Young Red thought. As a rule he was only interested in giving answers, showing off the brain-power he'd been told he had more of than most. Young Red concluded he was doing it to make Mouth jealous, excluding him from the relationship to get his revenge. But it never worked. Mouth was too cunning. He always turned the tables on everyone.

"No. I only know folks go to her when they have trouble of some sort. And... and she helps them." Young Red had said enough. Old Florrie's business was too private to talk about with the likes of Brock, with his tongue as loud as a bell-clapper.

"What you want to know about Wild Man for, Brockle-arse? Think some hairy bloke's going to jump out from a tree and grab you?" Mouth glowered at Brock, his face heavy with contempt.

"Only wild man down here's Young Shack. But, if you ask him, he might stick his two-two up your bum!"

Brock squirmed on the fencetop, looking down at the water. "I only want to know about the name. Could be important." He went on defensively. "Could be a very old name belonging to heathen times. Wild Man might have been a heathen god."

"Think he's stood at the wood end, just behind that hazel bush. Raggy's talking to him - look at him!" Young Red nodded towards the dwarflike figure, who sat several yards away from them.

They watched Raggy who was staring wide-eyed at the flood. He seemed to be communing with some unseen presence, the silent movement of his lips accompanied by animated gestures of his hands. Brock sniggered. "He's starting to give me the creeps. He ever done that afore?"

"Not that I know of." Young Red was also feeling uneasy. "He's mebbe going mad 'cos he's starving."

"Shit! He's mad 'cos he's Raggy! How many times do I have to tell you? It's in his sodding fam'ly - they're all a bit doo-lally!" Mouth's vehemence reduced them to an awkward silence. At his mention of food Young Red realised he was hungry.

"I'm going to have my dinner."

He produced a flattened meat pie from an inside pocket of his lumberjacket. This reminded Mouth and Brock how hungry they had become and assorted items of food were dredged from jacket pockets. Mouth watched Brock, waiting to taunt him about his polony sandwiches. One by one they made short pilgrimages along the fence to offer something to Raggy, because he hadn't brought any food at all. They watched as Raggy gobbled the food, nodding his thanks at them with his mouth crammed full.

Young Red finished eating and placed his pie case on the water, prodding it with the toe of his wellington and watching it drift slowly away towards the river on the indiscernible current. "Water's gone down another inch. Bottom fence-rail's showing."

Mouth finished his last cheese sandwich, tossing the crust over his shoulder into the trees. He had eaten his food without enthusiasm, giving half of it to Raggy, and all the while mocking Brock about the polony. Must have made his own sandwiches,

Young Red thought, because there's no-one else to make them. Bet he wishes he had some polony himself. Young Red knew Mouth pretended to hate what he coveted most of all.

Mouth glanced at the water in the wood. "Still too deep. Too many holes in there. We'll wait for it to drop a bit more afore we go into the wood. Tell you a story about Mawky, then we'll go."

"Mawson?" Young Red raised his eyebrows doubtfully. "You told us - arresting Harry Legge for being drunk in charge of his pushbike!"

"No - this happened last night. Ain't had time to tell you yet, have I?" Mouth cleared his throat and spat into the water. Young Red wondered if his friend was becoming bronchitic, like Mouth's uncle Sam. "Happened last night, afore my dad went off to the scrapyard. He was out with the dogs. You know - the ones we keep in the shed."

Brock and Young Red nodded. They knew the dogs in the shed were the ones Mouth's dad didn't take to illegal dog-fights. The fighting-dogs were moved around between countless secret locations that not even Mouth knew about. The dogs in the shed were a front.

"Well, my dad was out with a couple of old dogs in that field behind the hospital what belongs to Ginner Lund. And as he's walking he sees the dogs' ears go up and he stops to listen. And as he's listening he hears a sort of creaking noise coming from the field corner. Dogs are pointing it by this time, so the three of them starts walking real slow into the corner. And this creaking gets louder and louder till there's a great noise of grunts and squeals, like a load of pigs at feeding time. And my dad cottons on to what's happening and he lets go of the dogs and who d'you think gets up out of the grass but Mawky - and he's with a woman!"

"You're joking - in his uniform?" Brock was incredulous.

"He weren't on duty, you steaming shit! He were courting."

"What - Mawky? Who'd see anything in that long streak of piss?"

"Shut up and listen, Brockle-arse, or I'll only tell it to Red."

Brock looked down, pouting. He didn't want to miss out.

Mouth was a good storyteller, which was one reason for his nickname.

"Well, there was Mawky in his pacamac - it were his mac what my dad could hear creaking - shouting at the dogs and pulling up his pants and this woman - real scrubber my dad said - trying to pull her skirt down and put her shoes on and run away all at the same time, and Mawky were yelling that my dad had no right to be in the field and he'd report him for trespass and keeping dangerous dogs and my dad said he had more right to be there than anyone short of the owner and it were him - Mawky - what were trespassing and he'd better be glad it were only two harmless terriers and not the owner with his twelve bore and Alsatian or he'd be shitting blood for a month!"

They hooted and rocked on the fencetop until the structure started to sway and Raggy had to cling on to avoid falling backwards into the wood. He stared at them in surprise, which made them laugh even harder.

"Look at him, the stupid shit!" Brock gasped. "He ain't heard a word of it!"

Mouth stopped laughing and swung round on the fencetop, grabbing Brock by the collar with a long lean hand. "Who're you calling a stupid shit, you bloody hypocrite? You're nothing but a clever dick, who hasn't even got a prick, remember?"

"Pack it in, for Chrissake! Or I'll never come down to Wild Man again!" Young Red stepped down from the fence and retrieved his rifle from the oak tree. "Do that again and I'm off! I don't see why I should have to put up with you fighting all afternoon. You're frightening everything away and there'll be nothing to shoot at! Thought we were supposed to be having some fun?" He felt like thumping them both with the butt of the Airsporter.

"Okay, Red, don't get upset. Just you remember, Brockle-arse, not to say nothing about a kid what can't fight back. Must be even worse to be deaf than to be a fat prickless freak like you! Now give us a cig, Red, for all that talking."

Contrary sod, thought Young Red, still vexed. But he gave Mouth a Du Maurier.

They entered the wood following Raggy. Their advance was slowed by the tangle of roots hidden beneath the shallow water and the mesh of low branches that caught at their clothes and hair. Nothing appeared for them to shoot at and Mouth kept gesturing to them to go more quietly, much to Young Red's annoyance.

"You should have thought about that when you were rowing back there." He hissed angrily at Mouth. "You were making more noise than a bunch of praying women in the gospel church!"

Mouth scowled at him. "Shut up and keep your eyes open. There's a rookery further on and they'll be flying in and out all day feeding their chicks. We can just stand underneath and pot them off."

Eventually they shot a rabbit which had been stranded by the flood. Mouth handed the dead animal to Raggy.

"Here. For your supper. Tell your mam to make a stew. If we get to Willer Farm we'll nick you some taties from the shed to go with it." He turned to Young Red. "Might help him grow a bit if he has fresh meat."

"Better than ketchup butties."

Raggy beamed and croaked, stuffing the warm body into the big inside pocket of his duffle-coat.

Mouth seemed unable to locate the rookery. They stopped several times to listen, but the only birds' voices they heard were robins and wrens.

"They used to call the wren the king of the birds." Brock announced self-importantly. "'Cos it starts singing all day at midsummer. They used to shoot wrens at the end of December, 'cos that was when the robin took over. Then they shot the robins in the summer. Like in the rhyme about Cock Robin. I heard about it on the radio."

Young Red frowned doubtfully. Who cares anyway, he thought. Stuck up sod. Wrens were wrens whether you put them in a rhyme or not.

"Mebbe them rooks are nesting in another wood."

Mouth sat on a fallen tree trunk and scowled. "Give us a cig, then, Red, for all that walking. Then we'll go back."

"Gonna run out at this rate." Their vague meanderings were beginning to irritate Young Red. He felt the day was going to end in disappointment. He sat down heavily on the trunk next to Mouth. "Have to last us till Monday."

Brock settled himself in the ample fork of a crack willow, leaning back against the trunk and watching them with a knowing grin. "Gonna nick some more from Ralph's, then?"

Mouth had crossed the space between himself and Brock before Young Red had time to intervene. Brock toppled backwards from his perch and lay among the knotted roots, looking up in fright at the barrel of Mouth's rifle, which was three feet from the bridge of his nose.

"You say a word to anyone about what we do at Ralph's and I'll blow your fucking head clean off!" Mouth's face twitched with fury behind his rifle and he thrust the barrel closer to Brock's face. He shifted it slightly and fired. Brock screamed and rolled to one side, flinging his arm across his face for protection. The slug ricocheted from a root and pattered away into the leaves. Before Mouth could reload Young Red had grabbed his arms. "For Chrissake leave him alone! What we going to do if you kill him?"

Mouth lowered his gun and laughed. "Don't be daft. It ain't powerful enough to go through his thick skull!"

Mouth made to step back from Brock's prostrate form and Young Red felt obliged to release his grip. But he kept his eyes on Mouth's hands. He knew Mouth was at his most dangerous when he appeared to be backing off.

Mouth glowered at the figure on the ground. "You watch it, that's all, Brockle-arse. One word about us and Ralph's and you're dead polony! Remember that! Okay?"

Brock lay still among the lumpy roots, making no move to uncover his face. Mouth stood his gun against the willow, leaning one hand on the trunk and clearing his throat. Once more Young Red was too slow. Mouth's savage kick caught Brock in the small of the back and he screamed again.

"Leave him I said!" Tears of frustration stung Young Red's eyes. He felt the impotence of his rage in the face of Mouth's deviousness. "One of these days you'll do something that lands us both in big trouble!"

But Mouth only gave him a scornful grin and resumed his seat on the fallen trunk. Young Red sat stiffly some yards away and they smoked in silence for a while. As he inhaled the smoke Young Red felt soothed. He glanced at Mouth - the cigarette seemed to have made him calmer too. Smoking was good. It stopped folks going crazy.

A loud sniff came from the other side of the willow. Young Red looked at his watch. "Half past two. Better move on, hadn't we?"

Mouth stretched his long catlike limbs. "Sure. Get Brockle-arse." He looked around lazily then scowled. "Hey - where the hell's Raggy?"

Raggy had vanished. They stood up and peered into the trees. Nothing moved. The trunks of the alders rose dark and high around them, silent and inscrutable. They listened, but there was no sound except an occasional burst of song from a small woodland bird and the soft sighing of the wind among the year's first leaves. Young Red suffered a fleeting sense of his own insignificance, but it passed as quickly as it had come.

"For Chrissake, Mouth." He moaned. "We were supposed to look after him."

Mouth scowled. "We were doing. It ain't our fault if he goes off while we're resting."

"We should have made him stay near us. If you hadn't been fighting with Brock..."

"Bollocks! It's got nothing to do with me! I can't be watching him all the time. You said you'd look after him, so you should have sat with him!"

"I was stopping you from killing Brock!" Young Red stared at his friend gloomily. "He might have slipped in a bog or something..."

Mouth spat. "Nah. He would have shouted." He picked up his rifle.

"No good calling, he'd never hear us." Mouth's rubber face creased into wrinkled puzzlement. That's what he'll look like when he's old, Young Red thought. The old man's already inside his skin, waiting to take him over. They were all of them old already, unless they died young. He shuddered. Looking at Mouth just then had been like seeing his own future.

To break his sombre mood Young Red sprang into action. He found Brock, sullen and pouting, behind the willow and hauled him to his feet. "Raggy's gone off. We'll have to find him. He might bump into Upshot, or old Hardacre from Willer Farm. They might find the rabbit in his pocket and then there'll be all kinds of trouble."

In spite of his damaged self-esteem, Brock became infected with Young Red's sense of urgency and the three of them plunged together into the maze of alder trunks.

"Better split up," Mouth suggested. "No good going in a crowd like this. May's well be off on a rat hunt. Red, you work over to my left a bit, and you, Brockle-arse, you work on the right. Not too far. Stay in sight of each other. Shout if you see him. Okay?"

"How do we know he went this way? He might have gone back to where we had our dinner."

Brock's face seemed very pale and his freckles stood out like a rash. His mouth had a sour pinched look. Going to be a bitch when he gets older, Young Red thought.

"We don't." Mouth was thinking as he spoke. "We'll walk this way for fifteen minutes and then Red'll call stop, 'cos he's the one with the watch. Right, Red? And if we don't find him we'll turn round and go back to the fence. Okay?"

"And if we still haven't found him?"

Mouth spat into the trees. "We go home."

Young Red checked his watch. "Hope we find him. Don't want to go back home yet. My mam'll be ironing and my dad'll be shouting at her."

"Least you've still got them both." Mouth snapped savagely at his friend.

Don't know which is worse, them rowing or not being there, Young Red thought. But he didn't want to talk to Mouth about it.

They set off in line abreast, fifty yards apart. The flood had almost gone from this part of the wood, but it had left behind a slippery tangle of roots and ominous pools of uncertain depth. Young Red worked his way forwards steadily, picking his way between the pools, trying to keep Mouth in view to his right. Eventually he came to a stretch of water that entirely blocked his advance. It was so big - about twenty yards across - it was more like a pond. Which way should he go - to the right or the left? He chose the left, as it appeared to be the easier route. The trees seemed to shut him in and he felt the first signs of a headache. The vision in his left eye started to blur and he had difficulty seeing where to put his feet. He had not gone far when he caught his toe in a submerged knot of briars and almost dropped his Airsporter in the pool. Grabbing a willow branch to regain his balance he caught sight of a face staring up at him from the water. He blinked and looked again. The face had turned into a giant lily pad. Shit, he thought, it's Old Florrie again. It's that bit of me that's like her, that makes me see things that aren't there.

He stumbled around to the far side of the pool and found himself at the edge of an even bigger area of water. He realised he had reached the ponds that occupied the centre of the wood: fish ponds dug by the monks from the priory hundreds of years ago, some said. He had never been this deep into Wild Man before. He worked his way around the edge of the larger pond, wondering if it still contained any fish. He had heard somewhere that monks used to breed carp. When the monks died out the carp went on living, enormous and ancient, in the depths of mysterious ponds. Like this one. He stood at the edge of the pond, peering at the opaque water, wondering if the carp were too big to catch with a rod and line.

A big splash in the water six feet from the bank startled him. Carp! It must be! He crouched down at the edge of the pond, trying to reduce his bulk, so he wouldn't cast a shadow on the water and frighten the fish. Another splash to the right! And another! Jesus, the place was full of them! He stood up, thinking he should go and get Mouth fast and bring him here, before they lost contact with each other altogether, and there was Raggy on

31

the opposite bank, laughing silently, about to throw another stone into the water...

Mouth, Young Red and Brock followed Raggy deeper among the ponds. Mouth's sharp eyes noticed Raggy's coat was no longer weighed down by the dead rabbit. "Hey, Raggy, where you put that rabbit?"

But Raggy only grinned and gestured for them to follow him. Young Red observed, somewhat belatedly, that he had abandoned his blackthorn wand too.

They realised they were following a faint path between the ponds. Raggy seemed to know exactly where he was going. They looked at each other and shrugged.

"I smell smoke." Brock's nose twitched, Young Red thought, just like a rabbit's. "Raggy's gonna cook us our tea!"

The clearing to which Raggy led them took them by surprise. A fire burned in the centre, close to the opening of a rough shelter fashioned out of larch branches and moss. A figure was emerging from the shelter, carrying a big rifle with a telescopic sight and silencer. The figure straightened and stood very still watching them as they filed into the clearing.

"Now then, lads." They heard the quiet voice. "You're just in time for a spot of meat."

CHAPTER FOUR

Michael Shackleton, unshorn and unwashed, turned two skinned rabbits slowly over the fire. They stood around him, listening to the hiss of fat dripping into the hot ash, watching the constant movement of his hunter's supple hands: feeding the fire from a heap of sticks at his side, turning the meat, keeping the fire low and even, with not too much flame, nudging the small dry sticks one by one towards the glowing centre. He sat so still by the fire as his hands worked it was as if they were the only live part of him, like birds flying around a tree. No-one spoke. To be in Young Shack's camp - to be invited to eat with him - was an honour to be treasured.

Young Shack was the son of Jack Shackleton, the water bailiff. Old Shack lived in a crumbling cottage in the fields between Wild Man and the priory and, occasionally, Young Shack lived there with him. Mostly he wandered about with his rifle, pleasing himself, living off rabbits and pigeons and camping out in the woods when the weather was dry. Young Shack was a law to himself. Major Upsall, the shooting tenant, hated him, but the estate was happy to have him around as a kind of unpaid gamekeeper. Over the years Young Shack's presence had persuaded all but the boldest poachers to stay at home.

Not more than thirty-five, Young Shack was already a legend in the area. The tales of his woodcraft and cunning were many - and quite a few of them were true. But what impressed Young Red more than anything was his way of knowing things. Like the day in March when he had met him on the riverbank and Young Shack had simply said there was a bloke in Maple Avenue with an orange Carlton for sale. He had never told a soul he wanted a new bike... But the Carlton was perfect and he bought it. Then there was the time he and Mouth had met him at Wild Man and Shack had told them he was waiting for a jack hare that would be along in a couple of minutes. Sure enough the hare came galloping past the wood-end and Shack shot it with his big two-two.

33

To Young Red there was nothing Shack didn't seem to know. He knew how many owls were breeding on the estate and how many foxes. He knew if it would rain before evening, or if there would be a frost at dawn. He knew every bird's nest, every tree, every pool of water. And he knew about people, why they did things: why this man beat his kids, why that one was a drunkard. Whenever he met him, Young Red wished he could be more like him. Shack was in touch with the real world, with what mattered... But how could you become clever like that unless you just did what you wanted? Shack didn't have a father like Big Red, or a future apprenticeship at Reeds...

Young Red felt an affinity with Shack. He was awed by him, like the others, but he wasn't afraid of him. Even Mouth was afraid of Shack, he could tell... It was as if there was a deep bond, a warmth, between them, that he felt with no-one else. He felt it now, as he stood in the clearing watching Shack removing the rabbits from the fire and sprinkling earth to subdue the flames. He wondered if Shack sensed it too. It was a good feeling. Young Red's headache lifted and he began to feel confident and strong.

"Right, lads. One rabbit of yours and one of mine should make a feast for a pack of wolves like you." Shack cut up the meat on a flat stone with a big sheath-knife which Mouth watched covetously. "Sit where you like and enjoy it. If you come back in October you might get a taste of pheasant."

His bright brown eyes shone with good humour. Young Red responded to Shack's mood. "Not seen the Major today, Shack? Thought you might have asked him down for tea."

Soft spoken and never rushed, Young Shack always had time to talk.

"Major don't like water, you know. Prefers to drown himself with whisky in the Rose and Crown. Never comes this far into Wild Man. Too drunk to get this far in. Frightened he'll fall in a pond and that I'll just walk by and leave him." A faint smile hovered, as elusive as bird-shadow, over Young Shack's features.

"These ponds deep, then, Shack? Could you drown in them?" Brock cast an anxious glance at the dark surfaces on each side of them.

"My dad told me they were twelve feet deep. He measured them when he got the job here. Poacher fella called Matt Freer fell in one night and drownded." Shack's smile widened. "In there for a fortnight. When my dad found him he was blown up like one of them sputniks. Took four blokes to pull him out with gaff hooks."

Shack laughed quietly, spearing a piece of rabbit meat with the end of his sheath-knife. Mouth's eyes never left the knife as Shack took the meat carefully from the point of the blade with his teeth. Young Red noticed Brock had gone pale behind his freckles and had stopped chewing, sitting with his mouth full, staring at their host in horror. Raggy munched on, oblivious in his private world.

"What made him swell up like that, Shack? Do all drownded blokes swell up?" Mouth's eyes, as he spoke, followed Young Shack's knife as it speared another piece of meat.

"'Pends on how long they're in the water."

Young Shack picked the meat off the knife with his teeth. Brock turned away, surreptitiously removing the meat from his mouth and dropping it into the grass.

"If they're in for a few days or longer their gases can't escape."

"What gases, Shack?" Mouth kept his eyes on the knife.

"Well, the body's full of gas."

Young Shack took another piece of meat from the tip of his knife and wiped the blade carefully on his sun-faded corduroy trousers.

"You ask any of them undertaker fellas. When they have a dead body laid out it keeps farting and belching as if it were still alive. It's decomposing, see? Rotting away. And it makes gases that has to go somewhere."

Young Shack smiled at them benignly, but his eyes were as cunning as a polecat's.

Brock had gone white as a stoat in its winter coat and his freckles stood out like a disease. Young Red tried not to laugh at him and had to look away.

"So what happens when they drown, Shack?"

Young Shack stuck his sheath-knife in the earth between his

feet and ran his fingers through his mass of dark tangled hair.

"Well, the water fills up all the holes. Mouth, nose, backside -
the lot. And so the gases can't get out. As the body rots away
from inside the gases make it swell up. You know what they say
in the town, don't you - if a fella drowns in the river and no-one
can find him then he'll come up to the surface in a week. Well,
that's more or less true - any time from three days to a fortnight,
depending on the weight of the body and the amount of gas it
makes. Like that fella in the pond. My dad said he bobbed up
like a cork while he were stood there, and he was all swollen, as
if he'd been blown up with a pump. My dad said his skin was all
puffy and white, like that candy stuff you can buy at the fair."

Brock retched violently, doubled up and gasping. They
bellowed with laughter, Shack joining in. To Young Red's surprise
Mouth stood up and went to Brock's aid. As he passed Shack's
knife he loosened it with a casual nudge of his boot. Grinning,
he thumped Brock on the back.

"Get it all up and you'll be thinner. I told you afore, Brockle-
arse, you eat too much polony! If you don't stop you'll look like
that drownded bloke - and we'll have to get the vet to let the air
out of you like a sheep!"

"Piss off!" Was all Brock could splutter between gasps.

As Mouth returned to his place on the grass he again nudged
the knife with his toe as he passed. Shack was preoccupied,
retying the laces of his boots.

"Any carp in these ponds, now, Shack?" Young Red leaned
forward hopefully.

"Carp?"

Young Red explained, "Monks used to breed carp in fish
ponds. Thought there might have been carp in these. Great
massive uns, hundreds of years old."

"No carp. Might have been once, but there's no-one to feed
them now, is there?" Young Shack's reply was sharp. His mood
seemed to have suddenly changed. Young Red noticed it and
frowned, disappointed. He had hoped Shack might have
entertained them with tales about giant carp.

"If you can get that knife afore I do it's yours."

Startled, Young Red realised Shack's quiet words were addressed to Mouth. He watched Mouth's face as it registered the unfamiliar emotion of surprise. Mouth's eyes flickered to the knife, to Shack, then to the knife again. Both he and Shack were sitting on the grass, about six feet apart on opposite sides of the curved brown and gold handle. Mouth started to grin awkwardly, but the grin quickly gave way to a scowl of anger. He lunged for the knife, but his hand closed on air as Shack, with the speed of a pouncing cat, withdrew the blade from the ground and grabbed Mouth's wrist with his free hand. Their faces were inches apart. The faint smile was again flitting over Shack's face. Slowly, almost leisurely, he placed the flat of the blade on the end of Mouth's nose. Mouth squinted at the blade, his face blank with terror. Brock, recovered from his nausea, was agog at Young Red's side and even Raggy, his attention aroused by the sudden movement, was drawn in, mesmerised, to the edge of the strange tableau.

"Never start what you can't finish easily," Shack's quiet voice seemed loud in the sudden silence, "or someone else'll surely finish it for you."

He released Mouth's wrist, wiped the earth from the blade on his trousers and slotted his knife into the sheath on his belt. Mouth sat back heavily, clearing his throat. But he didn't spit, swallowing the phlegm with a grimace.

"You had me worried there, Shack," Mouth summoned the remains of his bravado. "Thought you was going to sharpen that blade on my nose!"

They laughed and the tension dissolved. Young Shack threw a handful of dry sticks on to the embers of the fire and produced a sooty kettle from the entrance of his shelter, placing it on the flaring sticks.

"Cup of tea now, lads, afore you go?"

They nodded, pleased there was no ill will.

"But I've only one cup so you'll have to pass it round."

They drank for a while in silence, sharing the cup. The dark unsweetened tea tasted of woodsmoke which, to Young Red, was quite pleasant.

"Tell us about Wild Man, Shack. Tell us how it got its name." Brock sounded positively chirpy. Mouth stared at him sullenly and Young Red wondered how long it would be before he got the beating Mouth couldn't inflict on Shack. Raggy sat some way off with his back to them, muttering to himself and tossing twigs into the water.

Young Shack, who had been squatting by the fire, rocked back on his heels, his eyes half closed.

"They named Wild Man after an old farmer fella what lived down here long ago." Shack prodded the fire with a stick, staring into the flames. "Well, he weren't much of a farmer - he just had this one cow and a few ducks and a fruit tree or two. One day he gets up and finds a bear has killed his cow in the night and he has no more milk to sell. Oh, dear me, he says, how am I going to live now I have no milk? But he's still got the ducks so he doesn't worry too much. A while later a fox steals his ducks in the night and he has no more duck eggs to sell. Oh dear, he says, how am I going to live now I have no eggs? But he's still got his fruit trees so he doesn't worry. A bit later on a couple of rough looking fellas come by and chop down his fruit trees in the night to sell for firewood and that poor farmer has no more fruit to sell."

Shack glanced at his audience and smiled. He ran his fingers through his hair.

"Now that old farmer thinks to himself, oh, so now I'm going to have to starve. So he goes to the duke who owns the estate in them days and he says your lordship I'm starving 'cos my cow was killed by a bear and my ducks were took by a fox and my fruit trees were cut down by thieves, please can you help me? No, I can't, says the duke. You should have been a better farmer. Go back to your cottage and starve. So this poor farmer goes to the monks who was down in the priory in them days and he says praise be to God, but I'm starving, 'cos my cow was killed by a bear and my ducks were took by a fox and my fruit trees were cut down by thieves, please can you help me? No, said the monks. You should have been a better farmer. Go back to your cottage and starve - but, if you pray hard enough, when you're dead your spirit might go to heaven. Then the farmer goes to the village which stood where the town is now and he says to the people I'm starving, 'cos my cow was killed and my ducks was took and my fruit trees were cut down for firewood, please can you help me? No, said the people. You should have been a better farmer. And they stoned him all the way back to the wood."

Shack threw a handful of sticks on to the fire and smiled at the three attentive faces.

"Well now, lads, if you was as quiet as this all day at school you'd be getting jobs as bank managers!"

"Go on, Shack," Brock urged, "what happened when the farmer got back to the wood?"

"Now don't you be rushing a good story, young fella. Stories are like friends. They get better with knowing slowly."

Shack prodded the fire with the stick. Young Red could hear Raggy muttering by the pond, but he didn't want to turn around and break the magic atmosphere Shack's tale had wrapped him in.

"Well that old farmer he ain't beat yet. He thinks to himself if no-one'll help me I'll have to take what I want. So he makes himself a bow and he makes himself a spear and he hunts the duke's game and he steals the monks' fish and he raids the village storage pits in winter. After a bit they find out who's doing all this and they set off to kill him. But that old farmer he's become a clever fella. He's taken to the woods and his cottage is empty and fallen to ruin and no-one can find him."

Shack paused again to hook the handle of the kettle with his stick and lift it away from the fire. He stared into the glowing ashes.

"And the village folk they search every path and track and clearing, but they still can't get a sight of him, 'cos that old farmer has grown his hair and his beard and he looks just like an oak tree covered with creepers. So they gets their hunting dogs and lets them loose, but the dogs can't get a hold of him neither, 'cos that farmer has become that clever with living wild in the woods he can make himself invisible when he wants. So they all give up and go back and they leave that old farmer alone. But, after a bit, they got used to him and they called the wood after him. And no-one knows if that old farmer died, 'cos they never found his body."

Shack glanced at the three spellbound faces, the faint smile creasing the corners of his eyes and mouth.

"And some say that old farmer's down here yet and you might get a sight of him early on a misty morning, drifting about like campfire smoke through the trees, making sure everything's all right in his wood."

Young Shack finished emphatically, "My dad told that story to me when I was a lad."

They applauded him. Brock was excited. "You seen that wild man down here on an early morning, Shack?"

Shack sprinkled a handful of earth on the fire. "I might have." The faint smile widened slightly.

"When my dad was down here on his own he told me he often used to think there was someone else about, sort of watching him. At first he thought it were poachers. But later, after he knew the story, he thought it might be that farmer fella. He never saw him, mind. It was just a feeling of not being alone. Of being watched, like."

"Wasn't your dad afraid?"

"My dad? Never!" Young Shack grinned. "My dad used to say that whoever or whatever it was that were down here it meant him no harm, 'cos he was looking after the place too, just like that old farmer."

Young Red tried one final time. "You're sure there's no carp in these ponds, Shack?"

"No carp, Young Red. Mebbe once, but not now." Shack laughed softly. "There's only dead men, now and then."

They left Shack in the clearing oiling his rifle and pushed slowly back through the trees towards the fence. They didn't talk much, as the going was difficult and they had constantly to change direction to find the easiest route through the tangle of branches and briars. When they reached the fence they perched on the top, drumming their heels against the middle rail.

Mouth spat into the shallow water. "Give us a cig, Red, for all that listening."

Young Red fished a crumpled pack of Du Maurier from his pocket.

"Water's gone down a lot. You can see all the bottom rail on the fence. Must have gone down at least three inches."

They sat on the fence and stared out at the receding flood. Brock picked thoughtfully at a spot on the back of his neck. "Wonder how Raggy found Shack? He were that hidden away I can hardly believe he could have found his way through to him just like that."

They stared along the fence at Raggy, who had resumed his private monologue.

"You think he sees things? You think he can see that old farmer bloke?"

"I told you afore, Brockle-arse, you steaming pile of crap! He's doo-lally! He don't know what he sees!" Mouth's face contorted into a scornful grimace. But there was fear there, too, Young Red could see it clearly: fear of the power of the madman. Since being with Shack Young Red felt much clearer about feelings. I'll be a wild man one day, he thought. It's better than working at Reeds.

Brock picked the spot on his neck. "Good story, though." He smiled at them self-importantly. "Told you there'd be a story about Wild Man. Now we know it too we can pass it on, like Shack did to us."

Mouth sneered. "Shack just made it up as he went along, you simple sod! Don't know why they think you have a brain - you believe every heap of shit people say!"

"I think it's true!" Brock pouted, colouring.

"So do I." Young Red stated firmly.

"You can believe what you like. I think you're both bleeding nuts!"

Brock smirked. "Well, why do you think it was called Wild Man?"

Mouth looked lost for a moment and Young Red feared for Brock's safety. He realised Mouth was jealous of Young Shack's talent for storytelling.

"It were called Wild Man after some old roadster fella what stopped down here for a month or two." Mouth grinned at Brock triumphantly.

"What's a roadster?"

"Don't you know nothing, polony head? Tell him what a roadster is, Red." Mouth stared at the flood with supreme disdain. Young Red felt a surge of relief.

"A roadster is a sort of tramp."

"A sort of tramp?"

"Someone who travels by road."

"You mean like a gyppo?"

"No. Like a tramp." Young Red struggled to think of words to fit the image in his head. "Someone who travels about and does stuff - cuts firewood for folks and fixes stuff that's broken. Mebbe sells kettles and pans, or else mends them. Used to be quite a lot of them about once, so my gran says. Mostly Irish."

Brock smiled patronisingly at Young Red. "You mean a tinker."

"What's a tinker?"

Brock looked smug. "Someone who travels about and fixes stuff that's broken. Mebbe sells kettles and pans, or else mends them. Used to be quite a lot of them about once. Irish fellas mostly."

"He must be a tinker then," Young Red struggled to keep his temper.

"Who must?"

"That roadster. The one they called Wild Man after." Young Red felt Brock was mocking him. Maybe he should let Mouth thump him after all.

"But they didn't. I thought you said you believed in the story Shack told?"

"I do!"

"But you just said they named Wild Man after a tinker."

"A roadster!"

Brock smiled condescendingly. "That's what I mean."

"What do you mean?" Young Red coloured. He felt Brock was reducing him to imbecility.

"I mean you don't know what you're saying!"

"Course I do! Wild Man was called after a tinker!" Brock was uproarious and Young Red was livid. "I mean a farmer!"

Mouth glanced at them along the fence then turned back to the shining flood.

"Like I said..." He spat into the water, "...like I said, you're both totally bleeding nuts!"

"Enemies at nine o'clock!"

Raggy's burnt out croak shocked them like a burst of gunfire. As if they were four quarters of the same being they leapt from the fence into the cover of the trees, snatching their rifles and crouching behind the screen of low branches. Raggy pointed distractedly through the trees.

"I see them." Mouth tugged Young Red's sleeve. "See? Three of them. Coming along the wood-edge. About three hundred yards downwind."

"Doesn't matter which way the wind's blowing, does it?" Brock put a slug in his old Original.

"They aren't rabbits - they can't smell us!"

"You're a sodding rabbit, polony head! And I'll put a slug right up your bum!"

Mouth lashed out at Brock with his boot but Brock was too heavily screened by protecting branches.

"Shut up and watch! There might be more of them!" Young Red loaded his Airsporter, peering between the railings of the fence. "They're kids."

"Don't recognise them. Must be from the council estate."

"They're younger than us."

"But they've got guns."

"So've we."

"And we've seen them first."

"Stupid sods - walking with their guns pointing all over like that! Should keep them low down against their coats. There ain't a pigeon in a mile could miss them!"

"They're easier to see than a windmill!"

Mouth pushed Raggy deeper into the trees. "Raggy - get down behind a tree, okay? You ain't got no gun. They might blow another hole in your pants!"

Young Red saw Mouth was about to take charge again after his eclipse by Shack.

"We going to ambush them?"

Mouth's lips curled into a malicious grin as he loaded a slug into his Webley. "Why not? Let's have a bit of fun!"

CHAPTER FIVE

Bent low they followed the inside of the fence, ducking under the branches of the trees. When they had reduced the distance between themselves and their advancing quarry to less than a hundred yards Mouth signalled them to stop.

"Aim for their legs and when they start running hit them on their backsides."

They crouched down, resting the barrels of their rifles on the middle rail of the fence. Ignorant of danger the three figures approached. They were youngsters of twelve or thirteen; each of them carried an air-gun, pointing at different angles into the sky. They laughed and joked, then imagined their rifles were tommy-guns and sprayed a burst of invisible fire into the trees. They capered about, pushing each other in the shallow water.

"Keep still, you pissing halfwits!" Mouth snarled behind the fence. "They're dancing about like bloody savages!"

The distance was reduced to sixty yards. The three boys were splashing along, watching the ripples spreading out from their wellingtons.

"Okay." Mouth hissed. "Take the one on the right, Red. Brockle-arse - yours is the one on the left. Okay? One - two - three - fire!"

They turned them with the first six shots, then vaulted the fence and ran after them, reloading and firing as often as they could. They kept them running the whole length of the woodside and out into the flooded fields.

"These are our woods, you young buggers!" Mouth yelled. "You're bloody trespassing!"

Brock and Young Red joined in.

"You keep out or we'll cut off your goolies!"

"We find you down here again we'll hang you by your fucking ears!"

They chased them through the shallow flood for half a mile. Their quarry screamed and stumbled and begged for mercy, completely losing their way in their panic and falling into hedgeside ditches. The three hunters stood back and waited while their victims regained firmer ground and then they shot at them again, driving them on like terrified animals. One of them dropped his gun in a ditch and another lost his cap. The hunters stood back and waited, laughing till their faces ached. Then they pursued them again, until they reached the line of poplars which ran towards the river from the fold yard at Willow Farm.

"Old Hardacre might be about," Brock gasped, breathing hard. "Better stop. He might have a go at us with his twelve bore!"

Mouth sneered. "Shit! We could run them for miles! Sod Hardacre!" He cleared his throat and spat at a poplar.

"No," Young Red, sweating, stared after the three fleeing figures. "Let them go. We've done enough."

"Two against one," Brock panted, too out of breath to provoke Mouth with his pompous grin.

"Shit! A pair of pussies is all you are!" Mouth glowered at them. "Better than shooting rabbits, ain't it?"

"We don't know what the land's like from here." Young Red gestured at the distant fields. "Could be deep spots. We might drive them into one and they might get drownded. Or we might."

Shack's description of the drowned man in the pond was still fresh in their minds.

"Okay." Mouth fired a shot at the disappearing figures. "They're out of range now anyway."

They waded through the fields towards Wild Man, their exuberance undimmed.

"See those stupid buggers run!" Brock giggled. "That one with the red hat that went straight into the ditch! Bet his hat's floated right down into town by now!"

Mouth grinned at his companions. "And that other with the black jacket! Yelling dad, dad, dad!"

"And that one that lost his gun! I shot him in his back and he stuck out his arms and let go of his gun just like a dying Indian!" Young Red flung out his arms in mimicry of his victim. Brock looked thoughtful.

"Should have gone back for that kid's gun. Might have been able to use it."

Young Red laughed. "Or sell it!"

"Nah," Mouth sneered.

"Only be a one-seven-seven. Won't even tickle a rabbit's bum with that!"

Brock stopped suddenly, looking troubled. "Think they know who we are?"

"No chance!" Mouth glared scornfully at Brock. "They was running away - not writing down a description!"

Brock seemed reassured. After a while his face brightened. "We was like Mau Mau - springing out at them stupid white settlers!"

Young Red was contemptuous. "Stuff Mau Mau! Mau Mau uses black magic - ju-ju and that. Don't need ju-ju when you have a bigger gun!"

"Shoulda been Upshot Bagley we was chasing and not just three stupid kids!" Brock looked aggrieved. "I'd give anything to put a slug up that bastard's nose!"

Young Red nodded. "If he weren't around we could do what we like."

"Well he ain't been round - and so we have!" Mouth spat at a gatepost as they passed.

"But..." Young Red objected, "he still has all this land."

Young Red thought how land ownership drove his father crazy.

"What you going to do, Red - hold him up and steal it like a highwayman?" Mouth scoffed. "Anyway, it ain't doing him no good. Blokes like that have always had too much and it don't mean a sodding thing to them. We can come down here when we want and please ourselves. He can't be everywhere. Better than fighting them."

Young Red looked at Mouth in surprise. He'd have to put that point to his father one day, he thought. But, then, it wouldn't make any difference. Nothing you said to Big Red made any difference.

Half way back to Wild Man they realised Raggy hadn't followed them. There wasn't a sign of him anywhere.

"He never came after us did he? Bet you he'll still be behind that tree!"

"He'll still be on lookout. Elephant at five o'clock!" Brock had a fit of uncontrollable giggles at his own humour. The others laughed with him. Brock beamed in self-appreciation.

"It's no use calling 'cos he'd never hear us."

"He might have got fed up with waiting and gone home."

"I wouldn't want to go home to all them screaming kids and no meat." Brock shook his head sagely.

"Ma Preston were saying his mam sends them out to pinch other people's washing, so they have enough clothes."

"Ma Preston'll say anything to start a fight," Young Red stated strongly, "She's an Evangelist."

His father hated Evangelists.

Mouth sniggered. "There once was a dame called old Ma Prest, she had warts on her chin and hairs on her chest; she were big as a barn and wide as a door, when she knelt down to pray her tits hit the floor!"

They held on to each others' shoulders and rocked with laughter.

As they arrived in the last field before Wild Man a strange sight greeted them. About fifty yards from the woodside, standing in a couple of inches of receding water, was a small figure in a torn duffle-coat. The figure turned slowly, its arms spread out and waving up and down, in a clumsy imitation of birdflight. It ran this way and that, flapping its arms, its mouth opening and closing soundlessly. It banked and wheeled like a gull, then it stood still with the ends of its arms trembling like a hovering hawk.

Afterwards, each of them accused the others of shouting the words, but each of them denied it. But one of them must have shouted, because all three of them heard it, "Hey, look! There's a wild man! A wild man - look! Let's get him!"

They set off running towards the flapping figure. The figure saw them and stopped gyrating. It grinned at them from its pitted face. Then the grin turned to a look of surprise. The figure cackled from its burnt out throat and set off splashing through the shallow water. Its three pursuers laughed too, leaping and prancing after it through the flood.

Who fired the first shot none of them could say. But, afterwards, each of them accused the others of being the first to pull the trigger. In the last analysis it didn't really matter. Someone fired a slug from his air-rifle and that was a signal to the others. The chase became a repeat performance of the earlier one, the three pursuers running, then stopping to shoot and reload, then running on after the shabby fleeing figure.

At first the figure ran a little, then turned, laughing and flapping its arms, then ran on a little more. After a while a look of alarm gripped its features and it turned and gestured to its pursuers to stop. But the three hunters came on and slugs zipped into the water around their quarry. The shabby figure started running again, no longer flapping its arms like a bird, but pumping them for all it was worth to go faster, faster, as the slugs zipped around it and the yells behind it grew wilder and louder.

In the second field beyond Wild Man the fleeing figure became confused. It missed the line of the field gates and turned south, into slightly deeper water. Its pursuers, caught up in their excitement, failed to notice the change in direction, but kept on running and shooting and yelling, oblivious of everything except the figure of the wild man that galloped ahead of them.

The wild man suddenly stopped and turned. The water was up to its knees. Frantically it signalled the three hunters to stop. Young Red, who was in the lead, saw the gesticulating figure and laughed.

"Now we've gotcher, wild man! We're gonna shootcher and hangyer from a tree!" Aiming for the figure's flapping coat he tripped on a submerged root and almost fell into the rushing water. He heard a cry as he regained his balance and, looking up, he saw that the wild man had disappeared.

"Fuck it, Red! You've shot him!" Mouth was at his side, then wading forwards into the deep swirling water in front of them.

Young Red checked his rifle. It was empty; the slug must have been fired.

"But, Mouth..." He began, confused, "it ain't powerful enough to shoot anyone..."

"Raggy has a thin head - you can see that!" Mouth spat into the water; his eyes were wild. "You can see it's half full of holes already!"

"But I didn't mean..."

"He's there!" Mouth was pointing, leaning forward, the water half way up his thighs. "I can see him, but I can't get him - he's drifting into the river!"

Brock joined them, but was too out of breath to speak. He stood gasping and wheezing, staring at the swollen flood before them. They could see Raggy, about ten yards off, lying face down and drifting further out. They edged forward, but the force of the flood near the submerged riverbank was astonishingly strong; the water filled their wellingtons, swirling threateningly around them.

"Oh, God. Oh, God." Brock's sobs rose to a shriek. "Oh, God! Oh, God! Oh, God!"

"Shut up!" Mouth roared, his face contorted with a mixture of horror and shock. "Shut up! Shut up, you fucking loony!"

As they watched Raggy reached a spot at the edge of the submerged bank where the water dipped and churned. He rose up on a boiling ridge and turned over. The three hunters could see a vivid red mark in the centre of his forehead. Then he entered the main current of the hidden river and was swept in a few seconds far out into the stream.

They backed out of the deeper water and headed for safer rising ground towards the hedgeside. They stared at the water and Mouth's sharp eyes picked out the floating form.

"He's there! He's two fields downstream already! We'll never catch him. We'll never..."

"He might get stuck in the weed below the Blood Hole and climb out."

A huge sob convulsed Brock's body.

"Water's too high. He'd never be able to..."

"He's dead." Young Red stated numbly, staring at the empty water. "Dead."

The clock at St Margaret's church was striking five as they reached the Roman Camp. They hadn't spoken on their walk back through the fields. Young Red could hardly drag himself along; his legs seemed as weak as willow twigs. He leaned on the fence below the camp and was sick. Mouth put his arm around his shoulders.

"Weren't your fault, Red." His voice was hoarse and rough, as if he'd caught Raggy's disease. "Could have been any of us... Just an accident."

Young Red nodded; he couldn't speak. But he felt far from reassured by Mouth's attempt to comfort him.

Brock wept quietly, leaning against the fence with his hands over his face. Mouth stood at Young Red's side, patting him on the back as he retched and gasped for breath. After a while they climbed the fence and sat on the grass, leaning back against the rails and looking towards the church. The sight of the old mellow stonework of the churchyard wall soothed them a little; none of them could face the view of the river.

Mouth was the first to break the silence, nudging Young Red's arm.

"Give us a cig, Red. It'll help me get home better."

Brock looked up at the church clock. "Shit! It's quarter past five! I have to go to the flicks tonight with my brother! Have to be there by half six. It's *Bridge On The River Kwai*," he volunteered, though no-one was interested. "What am I gonna do?"

Mouth's face was uncharacteristically vacant. "River what?" He asked absently.

"Kwai. It's in Burma."

Mouth cleared his throat and spat. "Fuck rivers!"

"But what am I gonna do?" Brock's voice rose to a squeak.

"You'll have to go, of course. Just act like nothing happened. Go home and have your tea and go to the flicks and say nothing to anyone about Raggy. Okay? We've got to protect Red 'cos it weren't his fault."

Brock nodded. "What you doing tonight?"

"Helping my dad get the dogs ready for tomorrer."

Mouth never went to the pictures.

51

"Where they fighting, then?"

"Dunno. Never know till I get there. My dad says it's insurance."

Brock prattled on. "My dad's taking us to the cricket tomorrer."

"He playing?"

"Opening bat. I might, too, if they're short."

Brock smiled unconvincingly at Young Red. "You going anywhere, Red?"

"To hell." Young Red answered flatly, staring glassily at the churchyard wall. An image of his father appeared in his mind, protesting that hell was a bosses' invention, but he dismissed him as if he was no more than an ignorant schoolboy. "I'm going to hell and I'll stop there for ever."

"For Chrissake, Red, we're in this together." Mouth insisted. "If we all say the same thing there ain't a problem." He stood up. "Let's go. Come on, Red, try and make an effort." He hauled Young Red to his feet and helped him stuff the Airsporter inside his jacket. "If anyone says anything about Raggy, just say he left us at twelve o'clock at the Roman Camp, okay?"

"There's Shack." Young Red said dully. His face looked haggard and he kept his eyes on the grass as he spoke. "And there's them three lads from the new estate."

"They never saw Raggy. Only us."

"There's still Shack."

"Shack won't say nothing. Anyway, it's our word against his. Three to one. If we stay together there won't be a problem." Mouth patted Young Red on the shoulder. "They won't miss Raggy for ages. It's Saturday - Ma Bottoms-up'll be on the barley wine from eight o'clock and she'll be sleeping it off all Sunday. Since Joe Bottomley left she ain't had a clue if her kids are out or in. It'll be okay. If Raggy goes falling about in the river it's got nothing to do with us."

"But we should've been looking after him..."

Mouth shook his head. "An accident, Red. It happens to folk every day. Cars. Planes. Fires. Floods. Hundreds of folk. Just another accident."

Young Red stared at his friend in amazement.

On the edge of the town they split up at Mouth's insistence and went home by separate routes. As he pushed open the backyard gate Young Red had a fleeting vision of his life from that moment onwards as an unending succession of ordeals. The first was tea and it was imminent. He hid his air-rifle in its usual place in the lean-to shed where he kept his new lightweight Carlton. Bracing himself as best he could he went indoors to change and wash the smell of the river from his skin.

CHAPTER SIX

Big Red and Nancy Patterson lived in a large terraced house close to the centre of the town. They had a bathroom, unlike the houses in the poorer streets, where Mouth and Raggy lived. The bathroom was a status symbol, which Big Red hated, but he spent half an hour in it each day after work nonetheless, saying it was easier than filling a tub in front of the fire. Easier for Nancy.

The Pattersons always ate in the dining room, which is what they called the room at the back of the house next to the kitchen. They never ate their meals with their plates on their knees, as some did, with their faces stuck to the telly. The television, which was in the dining room, was switched off by Big Red at six-fifteen prompt. Then the table was set with a clean flower-patterned cloth and the Pattersons, washed and combed, sat up to it expectantly. The front room, which they called the sitting room, was used only for special occasions, which hardly ever happened.

You could set your clock by Big Red. His gods were order and regularity. If he was late for his five-thirty bath it meant trouble at Reeds - and that meant the threat of a strike. Big Red was a foreman and shop steward at the town's steelworks.

As Young Red, smelling of talcum powder, stepped into the dining room Big Red turned the television off. Father and son glanced at each other and nodded.

"Had a good day, Dad?" Young Red tried to sound enthusiastic.

"Not bad. And you?"

"Not bad."

Young Red sat at the table and his father sat opposite. His sister was still getting made up in her room. She was always late for tea on Saturdays. Young Red wished Janet would be quick, he didn't like sitting alone at the table with his father. It was difficult under normal circumstances. Today it was unendurable.

"How long is it till you finish at senior school?" Big Red cast his heavy gaze across the table towards his son. Young Red felt it beamed at him, like some kind of futuristic weapon.

"Eight weeks. We break up on the twenty-fourth of July."

There was a long pause. Young Red stared at his empty plate.

"You'll be starting at Reeds on seventh of September. How many weeks is that from today?" Big Red beamed ponderously across the table. "Try and work it out in your head - quick as you can."

Young Red sighed. More of his father's cursed intelligence tests. Today of all days.

"Fourteen weeks and two days."

Young Red replied in a monotone. He knew the answer already. He was ticking off the days on the pocket calendar he kept in his bedside cupboard.

"And how many weeks is it till Christmas - till your first day's holiday?" Big Red's smile had slipped a little. A frown was slowly replacing it, inch by inch, like a dark flood.

Young Red was nonplussed; he hadn't prepared for this one. "Haven't a clue, Dad. Why?"

Big Red's heavy hands flopped against his thighs with a slap. He sighed with frustration. "And I thought you was improving. Can't you work it out?"

"We don't do stuff like that at school."

"What do you do at school if you can't work out a simple problem like that?" Big Red glared bullishly at his son. Should have a ring through his nose, Young Red thought resentfully.

"I've got enough problems," he heard himself saying, "without any more of yours!"

"Problems? What do you know about problems?" Big Red bellowed. "You sit there, a bloody nowt of fifteen and talk back to me about problems! You wait till you're working, till you have to take on the bosses every minute of the day - we'll see then if there's a man hidden away in you what can face up to real problems!"

Big Red's assault was cut short as Nancy opened the door from the kitchen and came in carrying a steaming tray. Her arrivals at the table were frequently timed to limit the effects of Big Red's wrath. Young Red glanced up at his mother and managed a weak smile.

His mother looked troubled and Young Red's heart did a quick backward somersault. Oh, Christ, he thought, were they searching for Raggy already?

"Where've you been all day, Ronnie? I've had Christopher Marsden waiting for you in the yard till two o'clock. He said you'd arranged to go for a bike ride out to the castle. I said you must have forgotten when you didn't arrive by two. He went away quite upset. You really must try to remember if you make arrangements with people. It's embarrassing for them - and for me - when this kind of thing happens. You've got to try to be more reliable."

She glanced a little tensely at Big Red. "You'll be starting work soon, like your father said. You won't be able to forget the time then."

"Sorry. I... I just forgot." Young Red tried hard to look suitably contrite. But he wished his mother wouldn't keep going on about his memory. In her way she was as bad as his father. Everyone knew he had a bad memory - there were countless occasions when arrangements with friends had completely slipped his mind. How could you fix a useless memory? It was like trying to dismantle the wind.

Janet appeared and took her place at the table. Young Red breathed a quiet sigh of relief. She was made up like a film star, he thought with distaste; he could smell her perfume through the steam of his stew and dumplings. Janet was nearly three years older than him and did things that were incomprehensible, like getting made up to go to the pictures. But he had always liked her, because she had always liked him.

"What d'you want to wear all that muck for just to go to the flicks?" He couldn't help accusing her as she waited for her stew. Janet tucked a large flower-patterned napkin into the top of her blouse. She pulled a face at her brother.

"I might be going somewhere else afterwards."

"Where? A nightclub? You ain't old enough to go to nightclubs!"

"I am too! Anyway it's not a nightclub. 'Sides, it's none of your business!"

"It is my business. You're my sister," he stated possessively, "I have to look after you."

He was reminded of Raggy then and wished he hadn't spoken.

"What - at Jack Parnaby's? I don't think you'd be very welcome there. They're all grown ups - and you're only the paper boy." Though she spoke kindly, it was an attempt to put Young Red in his place. But Young Red had the information he wanted.

"Ralph's lad's giving a party? You mean in the shop? Is he giving stuff away?"

Janet laughed, then hurriedly dabbed at her bright red lips with the napkin.

"Course not, stupid. He has his own house. One of them little cottages below the church in Cross Lane." She added in justification, "he's twenty-three. I met him on my way home from work at dinner time. And he just asked me. There'll be lots of other people there."

She glanced reassuringly at her parents.

"Jack says he has a party every week. Oh, yes..." She gave Young Red a secretive, knowing look, "Jack said he saw you today."

"I go down Cross Lane on my paper round. What's he doing - spying on me for his dad?"

"No, this was later. Jack said he saw you with three other lads below the Roman Camp mid-morning time. Said he could see you from his upstairs window. He said you were all stood looking at the river." Janet laughed. "It's that ginger hair of yours. You can't get away with anything!"

Young Red's stomach heaved and he thought he was going to be sick again.

"What d'you mean?" He asked defensively. "I weren't doing nothing! Just went for a look at the flood! No harm in that, is there?"

"Hey, steady on, lad - no need to shout!" Big Red boomed with his mouth full.

"Sorry."

Young Red felt he was always apologising. He was in a trap and he wasn't sure how to get out of it.

"I didn't mean..." He stammered, "I mean, I meant..."

"You weren't with that Leonard Dykes again, after all I've said?" His mother's worried face was pink and hot from the kitchen.

"He's a liar and a thief, just like his father! If the police don't arrest him for thieving they'll get him for fighting or causing trouble. He's bad from heel to hair! I've said this afore and you know it! You hang round with him and you'll hang with him!"

Young Red felt his world was in danger of going under.

"I weren't with him," he lied. "I mean, I was with Mouth for a bit, but then..." He blurted, all in a rush, "then I got fed up with him and went for a walk on my own!"

It was an obvious lie. Young Red lay on his bed after tea and cursed himself for his lack of presence of mind. But what else could he have said? This was a new situation and things were happening too fast. They just came at you from anywhere and you couldn't prepare for anything. The image came to him of Raggy, up to his knees in the river, signalling for him to stop. Then the water, stretching away for miles and Raggy gone. He couldn't believe he'd shot him. He couldn't believe it. He hadn't shot him - Raggy had just fallen into the water and floated away...

But there was that red mark on his head. He heard Mouth's words again, "Raggy has a thin head... You can see it's half full of holes already!" His slug must have gone straight through one of the holes in Raggy's head and into his brain. The shock of the realisation carried him to his feet and he clawed his way desperately to the bathroom and vomited his tea into the washbasin. He cleaned the sink and then his teeth and hoped the scent of toothpaste and scouring powder would mask the smell of sick.

No-one had heard him. His father had gone to the union club and his sister would be queuing up for *Bridge On The River Kwai*. His mother was washing up in the kitchen as the television played loudly to itself in the empty dining room. He couldn't face going back downstairs, couldn't watch telly, couldn't talk to his mother. She would know there was something wrong in a moment and he found it difficult to fake illness. He found it hard to lie, too, with conviction, whereas to Mouth and Brock it was the easiest thing in the world. But he couldn't stay in his room for ever; he would have to go downstairs soon. He would have to go out, to do something, or his mother would become suspicious and ask questions.

He lay on his bed and tried to think of Sally Bell, the sexiest girl in the senior school. But when her image came into his mind she had a terrible gaping hole in the middle of her forehead. She was standing at the edge of a cliff and signalling to him to stop...

He leapt to his feet and rushed to his bedroom door. But he froze, unable to bring himself to open it, and went back to sit on his bed. He moaned aloud and rocked backwards and forwards, hugging himself. After a while the rocking seemed to reduce his tension. He stood up and went to his dressing table mirror with the idea of combing his hair and going out. But as soon as he saw himself he had a renewed attack of anxiety. That hair, he thought miserably. "It's that ginger hair of yours. You can't get away with anything!" He cursed his father for giving him ginger hair. Why couldn't he have had black hair like Mouth's dad, or fair hair like Brock's? Why ginger, of all the stupid colours to have? He wondered how many other people, besides Jack Parnaby, had recognised him from their upstairs windows as he followed Raggy through the flood below the Roman Camp. He had the notion of shaving his head, but a baldheaded youth of fifteen was even more conspicuous than one with ginger hair...

He sat down on his bed. Again the image of Raggy filled his mind. Raggy looking up at the dead coot in the tree and croaking "Dead... dead." And now, so soon after, Raggy was dead like the coot... Raggy throwing stones in the pond, that he had thought were jumping carp... Raggy smiling, beckoning them to follow on the path that led to Shack's camp... Raggy eating roast rabbit... Raggy fleeing through the water pursued by three insane hunters... Raggy turning over in the river like a log, with that bright red mark on his head...

But how could such a glorious day end up like this? How? Raggy couldn't be dead. He just couldn't be... He would have floated down the river and got caught in the weed below the Blood Hole, like Brock had said. Then he would have drifted in to the bank and climbed out. There was a series of old landing stages on the riverbank below the Blood Hole, from the days when there were more boats and the riverweed was regularly cut. Raggy would have found a landing stage and climbed out. And if, by some stroke of bad luck, he had somehow died in the water he would be stuck in the weed below the Blood Hole anyway. He thought of what Shack had said. But Raggy was small - it shouldn't take four blokes to pull him out.

A desperate plan was forming in Young Red's mind. He went out of his bedroom and stood on the landing listening. He could hear the TV in the dining room; laughter and loud voices. His mother must be watching a comedy show; on her own, as usual, till the rest of the family came in for supper. He glanced out of the landing window - still about an hour's daylight left. There was no hurry. He didn't want to be seen doing what he had to do.

As quietly as he could he opened his parents' bedroom door, crossed the room quickly and opened the wardrobe. There, as he expected, was his father's best Sunday cap, hanging on a hook inside the door. He took the cap out and left the room. Back in his own room he put the cap on and looked at himself in the mirror. That was better. The cap felt odd because he wasn't used to it, tight and restricting like a bandage; but it covered most of his hair. In fact, he looked quite different in a cap. Normally he would never have considered wearing one, because it placed him in what Mouth derisively called the flat cap brigade; the workers, the wage-slaves whom Mouth scorned. It reminded him that, all too soon, he would become one of them himself... But tonight was different. Tonight it would serve a more important purpose; it would hide the Belisha beacon of his hair.

He rejected the check-patterned lumberjacket he had been wearing all day and put on a nondescript dark blue cotton windcheater with a zip-front and high collar. He stuffed his father's cap inside his jacket, fastened the zip and went downstairs. He opened the dining room door just wide enough to get his head inside the room - he didn't want his mother to see the bulge in his jacket which covered his father's cap.

"Just off out for a ride round on my bike." He had to shout over the racket of the television. "Back by ten."

He took his lightweight racer from the lean-to shed in the yard and then, most important of all, the gaff-hook, which stood against the wall in the corner behind his fishing box. He fastened the gaff-hook underneath the crossbar, with the hook-end almost hidden beneath the saddle. Closing the backyard gate he put on his father's cap and turned up his jacket collar. Suitably prepared he cycled, by a circuitous back lane route, across the town towards the river.

The street lights were coming on as he approached the bridge, but it still seemed nowhere near dark. Had he left it too late? Would there be enough daylight to see what he was doing? But if there was too much light he would be too visible... He hoped he had timed it right.

He was relieved to see that the bridge was deserted. Everyone was either in the cinema or the pubs. As he crossed the bridge he could hear the muffled thunder of the floodwater raging underneath. On the far side he dismounted and lifted his bike over the stile at the start of the riverside path. He didn't look around. Pulling his collar up and his cap down he climbed quickly over the stile and vanished into the shadow of the bridge.

The water was still high, about six feet above normal, he reckoned, to judge by how far it came up the piers. It surged beneath the bridge with a hollow roar, like some ancient beast let loose upon the town. Young Red could hardly bring himself to look at the river. He hid his bike in a clump of tall weeds and set off along the bumpy path.

The floodwater was about a yard below the path, though it had covered it earlier in the day, leaving behind a long line of shallow puddles, which glimmered in the evening light, and a treacherous surface. Young Red leaned on the handle of his gaff-hook to keep his feet steady as he hurried downstream as fast as he dared. The water boiled and foamed below him and he could hear nothing above its roar. It was growing darker by the minute and he started to feel unequal to the task he had set himself. He had never felt so desperately alone.

He reached the Blood Hole and stared across the sullen flood at the back wall of the slaughterhouse. The big black sluice-pipe that emptied the blood from the killing floors into the river gaped at him grimly. No riverweed ever grew here - the current was too strong. He hurried on downstream, away from the town, towards the old landing stages, where the river widened out and grew more sluggish.

In the half-light Young Red spotted the first mats of weed trailing in the water like drowned hair. There was the first landing stage - and there was another. He stared at the water, then ran his eyes along the banks, hoping and dreading he would find what he had come for.

As he walked he was beset by surges of panic. Each time the feeling rose he glanced back at the lights of the town. The lights reassured him. Beneath the lights were streets and people, the things he had always known. He plodded doggedly on through a darkening world of water and willows, gripping his gaff-hook tighter, staring at the river, peering beneath the landing stages. Hoping and dreading; dreading and hoping.

At the last but one landing stage something was lying in the water. A dark humpy sort of thing. A blob of deeper darkness on the rapidly darkening water. Not big - but large enough... Young Red's legs had turned to water too and he leaned against a willow for support. He wished Mouth was with him. Mouth would scorn his timidity and go forward. Well, he was as bold as Mouth. He had proved it often, when he had been pushed.

The humpy thing in the water was caught in the angle of the landing stage and the riverbank. In the half-light it looked like a body... It was a body! Swollen up, like Shack had said, but almost completely submerged. Kneeling on the landing stage, his arms and legs trembling, Young Red tugged at the body with his gaff-hook to try to make it move so he could see its head. The point of the hook tore into the soft tissue and Young Red almost let go of the handle in disgust. The stench that hit him was unbearable

62

and he cried out with shock and revulsion. Clenching his teeth he tugged again and the head came to the surface.

He shrieked in horror as the skull came into view. But it wasn't quite like the way Raggy's head should be... As he stared at the thing in the water he realised slowly what it was. It was the body of a long drowned sheep.

Young Red stumbled back along the riverside path towards the town. It was dark now and the street lights dazzled him, so that his progress was painfully slow. But his visit to the river had been worth it. He knew if there had been a body caught in the weed he would have seen it. Raggy must simply have climbed out and gone home. It was impossible to deny that there were alternatives. Raggy could have got hooked up on the low branch of a tree; he could have been beached as the flood receded. He could turn up anywhere from the riverside below the Roman Camp to the Blood Hole - a distance of almost two miles. The river could simply dump him below the bone mill, or by the bacon factory wall. If it did he would be found quickly and the cause of death would become known.

Young Red stopped suddenly and stood still as the truth sank in. It would be murder - and he was the murderer.

The church clock was striking ten as he tugged his bike free from the clump of weeds by the bridge. As he set it down on the other side of the stile he saw in the light of the streetlamps that the back tyre had gone flat. Entirely flat. Oh, damn, damn, damn! A puncture was all he needed to complete the worst day of his life. He had taken his pump off and left it in the shed, clipping the gaff-hook on in its place. He had no choice but to walk the half mile back home. And he would have to hurry, or his father would be back first and might notice his best cap had gone...

He pushed the Carlton across the bridge and past the locked gates of the dyeworks. On up the deserted street past the feed mill and the brewery. The vast bulk of Reeds loomed on the corner; above its enclosing walls Young Red could see the glimmer and flash of the furnaces. He hurried along the pavement breathing sulphur. On the opposite corner the Black Swan was ablaze with light; laughter washed over him from its doorway, taking him by surprise. Laughter belonged to other people's lives - it had no place in the shadow-world of a murderer.

He turned into the main street and almost fled in panic. The cinema was emptying and he had to push his bike right past it. He had no time to use side streets and alleys, as he had to be back before his father got home from the club. But he still had on his disguise and he hoped no-one would recognise him. He crossed the road and walked quickly on the opposite side from the cinema entrance. People were pouring out on to the pavement. A chorus of shouts assailed him.

"Hiya, Red! Taking your bike for a walk?"

"Great film, Red! Shoulda come. You wanna go for a coffee?"

"Nice hat, Red. Suits you. You going to work?"

He saw Brock coming out with his brother and their eyes met. He waved nervously, but Brock just stared straight through him as if he wasn't there. Perplexed, he hurried on, arriving home five minutes before his father.

He went to bed without talking to anyone. His sister was still out at Jack Parnaby's party and his parents were having their usual Saturday night row in the kitchen. As he took off his trousers he realised they were covered in rivermud. He looked at his hands - they were filthy and, when he sniffed at them, they stank of dead sheep. He rushed to the bathroom and spent a long time washing them. He washed them again and again, but each time he raised them to his nose he thought he could still smell the sheep. He shook some of his sister's perfume on them in the end. He hated the perfume, but it got rid of the smell of death.

He couldn't sleep. The smell of the perfume was bothering him and, as he got used to it, he imagined the stench of the sheep had come back. Then he thought that it was his own body that was smelling, because he had become contaminated with death. He had been wading through death for hours and had become saturated with it.

Eventually exhaustion carried him into sleep. He woke up several times, his head in a strange turmoil. In the middle of the night he dreamed: he was crossing a river, not by a bridge, but by following a line of stepping stones. Then, when he was only half way across, the stones became the bloated bodies of drowned sheep.

He gasped and woke up in his sweat-drenched, scented bed.

CHAPTER SEVEN

The Swamp was a wasteland of wild grass and willows at the back of the senior school. Twenty years earlier it had been allotment gardens, where taciturn men in overalls spent long hours making fences for runner beans and regretting their marriages. In 1940 a German plane had overshot its target and bombed it, so the allotments had moved, leaving the remains of the old sheds to be dismantled slowly by the wind. At night it was a place for prowling tomcats. During the daytime, in dry weather, the older pupils in the senior school escaped there and a tradition of clandestine liaisons and violent plots had developed in its atmosphere of abandonment.

At the far side of the Swamp from the school was the river, hemmed in between crumbling floodbanks, narrow and fast. Occasionally, in winter, the water spilled over and the bomb craters became ponds, submerging the used condoms and empty lemonade bottles of the summer. In late May the place was almost pleasant, with the willows in fresh leaf and the litter hidden by the year's new growth of grass.

The freak flood of three days ago had receded, but it had breached the inadequate defences and the grass steamed in the sun, giving the place the appearance of a tropical wilderness.¯

A gap in the schoolyard fence led straight into the Swamp. At twelve-thirty on the Monday after the flood three figures slipped through it and threaded their way between the craters towards a clump of willows. They disappeared among the leaves and the place was deserted, apart from the solitary figure of a young blond girl, who wandered through the grass pressing a transistor radio to her ear as she ate a sugar sandwich.

"Belly's come out to parade herself in the sun." Brock eased himself on to an empty oildrum and took his lunch from his pocket. "Listening to her sodding music - you'd think they never did anything else on the radio."

"What's she got to do with you, Brockle-arse? Belly's for men. Not soft lumps of polony like you! Me and Red'll get round to

Belly later." Mouth found another empty drum. "More important things to do today." His rubber face creased into a mass of troubled lines, like an ancient tribal mask. "You okay, Red?"

Young Red was searching in the grass. Eventually he located the old wooden box he often sat on and dragged it over to the others.

"Someone's moved my box." Young Red looked a little pale and smelled faintly of perfume. He took a pie from his pocket and sat down, glancing at Mouth. "Had a bad night on Saturday. Bad dream. But yesterday was all right. Went for a bike ride with Chris out to the castle. He's got a new racer."

He took a small bite of his pie and chewed it mechanically. Mouth unwrapped his bread and cheese and started pulling off the crusts, throwing them into the grass. Young Red glared accusingly at Brock. "Why didn't you speak, you moron, when I saw you Saturday night?"

"'Cos I thought you was in disguise."

"How did you know?" Young Red looked at Brock in surprise.

"'Cos of your hat. You never wear an hat."

Young Red wondered if everyone else outside the entrance to the cinema had thought he was in disguise too.

"Just felt like wearing it. It's my new hat for Reeds." As he spoke a vision of the steelworks reared up in his mind, its high blank walls like a prison.

"Anyway..." Brock spoke with his mouth full. Young Red could see bits of chewed food between his teeth and looked away, feeling queasy. He looked at the pie in his hand and felt worse. Brock continued, wiping his mouth on the back of his hand. "Anyway, I've decided you're not my friend any more and so I'm avoiding you."

"Since when?" Young Red felt the stab of a new wound.

"Since Saturday night. I told my mam and dad I was fed up with you." Brock hesitated, uncertain if he should go on. "And with Len - they don't like me to call you Mouth - and I said I'd be spending more time with them. We had a good day at the cricket. I got sixteen and a catch." His boast sounded lame and flat.

"Suits me, Brockle-arse. You're nothing but a pussy, anyway." Mouth's features transformed themselves from indifference to mocking contempt. "Shoulda been a girl and then me and Red coulda screwed you." He added savagely, "That is, if you'd been better looking."

"Screw you!" Brock stood up. "I don't have to sit here and be insulted by a sodding moron!"

In spite of his gloomy mood, Young Red was alert enough to lunge between Mouth and Brock to prevent what he was certain would be a second tragedy.

"For Chrissake! Can't you do anything but argue? You're worse than my mam and dad! We're supposed to be here for a talk - not a bloody fight!" He scowled at them both until they had sat down again. They were silent while Mouth finished his bread and cheese. Young Red struggled through half his pie and hurled the rest into the willows.

"Now give us a cig, Red. It'll help me think better."

Young Red opened a fresh pack of Du Maurier, waiting for Brock to say something about pinching from Ralph's. But Brock had sailed close enough to the wind for the moment and was content to chew noisily on a halfpenny square of bubble-gum.

Mouth and Young Red smoked in silence. Again Young Red noticed the calming effect of the cigarette. It seemed that his raw nerves were being bandaged with soft spirals of smoke.

"They never found him yesterday, then?" Mouth opened the batting with a tentative prod. Young Red shrugged.

"Would have been all round school if they had. Cathy Raines' gran lives opposite Bottomleys. She would have seen the police arriving - she stares out of her winder all day long."

"Pity we don't know anyone at the deaf school. If he wasn't there we'd know he was definitely killed." Brock was unable to meet Young Red's eye. Mouth studied the scuffed toecaps of his boots.

"He ain't at school. I saw his brother on my way back from my papers and he said he must have run away to sea, 'cos he ain't been home since Saturday. I said how did he know and little Billy said he knew 'cos that's what he always said he was going to do. I said mebbe he's gone nicking and Billy said no, 'cos he don't go nicking in his wellies."

There was a long silence following Mouth's revelation. After a while Brock announced huskily, "So he must definitely have been drownded."

No-one spoke again for several minutes. Young Red ran his fingers distractedly through his curls. He tried to cheer himself up with a new idea.

"He might have got washed right through the weed and been carried downstream. He might have just kept on going and be out at sea by now anyway." He looked at Mouth for confirmation.

"No bloody chance! There's weirs and old broken locks and a tide-barrage and all sorts afore you get to the sea." Mouth spat into the willows. "He'd never get through all that without being spotted," he looked at his companions' blank faces, "I've seen it." He explained, "Been that way with my dad. We can go fifty miles off on a Sunday for a fight."

Young Red looked agonised.

"Where's he gone, then?"

Mouth stared at Young Red as he spoke. It seemed Mouth had become somehow stronger since their day by the river. Stronger - while he had grown weak and unsure.

"He ain't gone nowhere. He's right here. In the river... in town."

Young Red felt that the blood had been syphoned out of his body and replaced with something like melting snow. He felt a chill spreading through him, as if he had died, but was still alive. He made an effort to try to think.

"He could just turn up, then?"

"His coat must have soaked up a lot of water. And his wellies'd fill up too. They'd have dragged him down to the bottom 'cos he's light. He mebbe floated for a bit and then went down. I bet he's between the bone mill and the Blood Hole. Been working it out." Mouth nodded in confirmation of his calculations. "Bet he's under that deep weed by the bone mill siding."

"How long'll he stay down there?" Brock had started to fret. He seemed, to Young Red, to be about to weep. If he made his eyes all bloodshot and sore someone in class would notice.

"Who knows? Like Shack said it depends on how big he is, and how much gas he can hold." Mouth's features creased with concentration as he conjured with imponderables. "He was only little, so mebbe a week, not much more. When he comes up he'll start floating and the blokes loading the railway wagons'll see him."

"My dad checks that siding line once a week. He might be there when they find him." Young Red was dimly aware that Brock was chewing his bubble-gum faster and faster. "What'll I say if he comes home and tells me?"

"You don't say nothing at all." Mouth glowered at Brock. "You just listen to what he has to say and come and tell me and Red."

"But..." Brock began to protest. "But you're not my friends any more. I told my mam and dad I was fed up with you!"

Mouth stood up. Maybe he'll strangle Brock now, Young Red thought, but he felt too tired and depressed to care.

"Listen, Brockle-arse," Mouth leaned menacingly over the freckled face. Brock stopped chewing and stared up at Mouth with an expression of defiance. "I keep telling you, polony brain, we're in this together. Me and you and Red - get it? You chicken out and I'll beat you into shit!"

Brock stood up too and took a step backwards. The oil drum fell over and rolled into the grass.

"But it's got nothing to do with me! I was a long way behind and I wasn't even shooting! I were just trying to keep up with the rest of you!"

"Lying sod!" Mouth swung his fist savagely at Brock's head, but again found Young Red intervening, gripping his arm.

"Don't hit him." Young Red spoke urgently into Mouth's ear. "If you hit him there'll be blood and the teachers'll want to know what happened."

Mouth spat into the grass, but made no further move.

"One of these days, Brockle-arse, I'll be waiting for you. You'll have to look over your shoulder for the rest of your shitty little life!"

Brock backed out of the willows.

"I'm not your friend! I wasn't there! It's got nothing to do with me!"

"Two against one, Brockle-arse!"

"I don't care! They'll all believe me - 'cos I'm not a troublemaker like you two!"

"You shit! You slimy little shit!"

"Let him go." Young Red held on to Mouth's shoulders. "If you go chasing him he'll blab it all over school."

"We ought to kill him and dump him in the priory well!" Mouth stepped to the edge of the willows with Young Red close behind.

They watched Brock cross the rough grass and disappear through the gap in the school fence. "So much for talk! Nothing's been sorted."

"I went down the river Saturday night. To the landing stages. All I found was a drowned sheep. But I'd have seen him if he'd been there."

"Like I said - he's still upriver. But too near the town to do anything about it. If he comes up we'll just have to deny it."

"Brock'll blab - sooner or later."

Mouth spat. "Mebbe."

"If he's been in the water a week will they be able to tell he was shot?"

Mouth shrugged. "Dunno. If Brock blabs they'll look."

Another plan was forming in Young Red's mind.

"If we found him first and cut off his head and buried it no-one'd know."

Mouth stared at Young Red in horror. "Jesus, Red, you give me the fucking willies!"

Young Red shrugged. "It was just an idea."

As they left the shelter of the willows they stepped straight into Sally Bell clutching her radio.

"What you snooping here for, you stupid cow?" Mouth snarled into her face. Sally Bell shook her silky blond curls and stuck out her tongue.

"I'm not snooping!" She pretended to sulk. "I just wanted a cig."

Mouth had slapped her across the face before Young Red could stop him.

"How much you heard? How much you heard, you stupid bloody cow?"

Sally Bell burst into tears. Her eye make-up started to run down her cheeks.

"Nothing. Only - "

"Only what?" Mouth raised his hand again. Sally Bell cowered and whimpered in fright. She hugged her radio to her chest.

"Nothing! I ain't heard nothing! I've been listening to my radio. Honest. Honest!"

Mouth studied her critically, as a dog-fighter might appraise a new breeding bitch. He glanced at Young Red and a silent understanding passed between them.

"Give her that spare pack of cigs, Red."

Young Red handed Sally Bell an unopened packet of Craven A.

"Thanks, Red." Sally Bell dried her face on the back of her hand, smudging her make-up. Young Red gave her his handkerchief. Thanks. You want to come down the priory tonight?"

"No." Young Red looked at her sternly. "You want to forget every word you heard in them bushes?"

Sally Bell smiled coquettishly. "You promise to get me some cigs when I want?"

Young Red looked at Mouth and the unspoken agreement passed between them again.

"Okay."

"Promise?"

"Promise."

Young Red lay on his bed after tea and tried to make sense of the mess his life had become. Less than three days ago things had been okay. He had been a better than average pupil in his last term at the senior school with a better than average future as an apprentice at Reeds. He had been set on a course that would take him right through his adult life. There would be problems, of course, but nothing too extreme. The occasional strike. The odd row with neighbours or family. Concern about health and money. Like everyone else.

In the space of a few crazy minutes he had wiped all that out and become a murderer.

Three days ago, when he was bored, he would have gone down to the yard and cleaned his air-rifle. Now he couldn't bear to think of guns - the Airsporter in the shed was as untouchable as a nest of vipers. Three days ago he would have gone down and sorted through his fishing box, getting his tackle together for the start of the season. He couldn't think of fishing. Fishing meant rivers, where dead things waited in hiding.

Three days ago he had friends and a family. Now he could trust no-one. What about his parents, he wondered - should he tell them? But there was nothing to tell: Raggy had not been found. With luck he might never come up. Or he might float through the weirs in the night... If they could

only keep Brock and Belly quiet... Anyway, if he told his parents Big Red would virtually disown him; and his mother would nag him to death for the rest of his life.

And the town would shun him. Everyone would avoid him. When he came out of gaol he'd have nowhere to go. No-one would speak to him ever again. He'd starve. He'd die in the gutter like an unwanted dog.

There was Mouth. Only Mouth. The troublemaker everyone hated. The fact that Mouth was on his side made it worse. Mouth was a liar and a thief. No-one would believe a thing he said.

Mouth had fallen out with Brock and now Brock had become their enemy. Soon they would find the body and Brock would tell. He might have told his parents already... Brock didn't smoke - he hadn't accepted stolen cigarettes from Ralph's. He didn't go with girls. There was nothing they could scare him with. Brock would say it was them and everyone would believe him. Because Brock was good at school. Because he didn't cause trouble or steal or go with dirty girls.

Brock was the one person that he really feared. Brock was the person that he hated most in the world. Mouth was right: they should kill him and throw him down the old well in the priory. But how?

Then there was Sally Bell. How long had she been snooping? Had she heard them arguing in the bushes? He didn't believe she had been listening to her radio, because when they had caught her the radio had been switched off... Would she talk to her friends? Would she talk to that aunt she lived with on the new estate? If they stole cigarettes for her to keep her quiet how many would they have to steal?

There was Jack Parnaby who had seen them from his window. There was Young Shack. There were the three lads they had chased. He had red hair, which was worse than being naked. He had been seen in disguise, which was worse than being seen with red hair...

He couldn't sleep. He couldn't eat. He couldn't put his mind on schoolwork. He couldn't cope with his father's stupid intelligence tests. He couldn't think. He couldn't make sense of anything.

Still, they hadn't found the body.

But they would. It was just waiting in the future like an assassin. And then Brock would tell.

The house at the end of the steep cobbled street was different from the rest of the terrace that was attached to it. It was older and the front door and windows were in a different style: the doorway was shorter and wider and the windows had a greater number of much smaller panes. The house was also a few feet lower than the others and had a roof of discoloured pantiles, not slates like the rest. It was a cottage, that had once stood on its own at the top of the little hill and, as its owner often remarked, it had once had a view of countryside. But the terraces and factories had closed it in, until its creamy sandstone had been eaten away and gone black and its owner, who had steadfastly refused to move, had become more and more secretive and strange.

There were no lights in the front windows - there never were - so Young Red pushed his bike around the end of the block to the yard. He stood for a moment in the dusk, looking down the deserted back lane. There was an old van with a smashed windscreen, a bikeframe with no wheels, a burst football, overturned dustbins, dogdirt and litter. About ten houses down, tied to the handle of a backyard gate, a yellow mongrel scratched and whined. Mouth lived in the next street. It was the poorer end of town.

He tried the latch of the high backyard gate and, to his surprise, it opened. He lifted his bike over the step and slipped quickly into the yard. There was a light downstairs so he knocked on the back door and waited. He listened while unseen hands struggled with bolts and a key. The door opened an inch and a shaft of yellow light cut the dark yard in two.

Young Red stared at the crack of light. "Hello, Gran. It's Ronald. I've come for a reading. I want to know if the future's going to be okay."

"Come in, lad." The voice was too strong, too big for the tiny frame that greeted him in the doorway. "I always unlock the gate about now. That's when they come, y'see. They won't come in the daylight. You're the first one tonight."

He followed her into the yellow light, which came from a paraffin lamp which stood at one end of a dining table. It was the first time he had been to see Old Florrie so late in the day. When he was smaller he used to come a lot with his mother, but they always went into the front room. His grandfather had been alive then and things hadn't seemed odd at all. He had never come in the back way, or stood in the room with the yellow light.

"Have they cut off your electric, Gran?"

It often happened in that part of the town.

"No, lad. But I can't see with it. That old lamp's a better light for seeing. Now if you sit at that table I'll make us a cup of tea and then we can get started."

She disappeared into the cellarhead kitchen, but was back in a few moments with a tray. The tea must have been made already, Young Red thought. She must have been expecting someone else.

Mystified by Old Florrie's strange talk Young Red sat at the table sipping his tea. The room did seem a little peculiar - what bits he could see of it in the pools of soft yellow light between the chasms of shadow. The walls were crammed with photographs - and there must have been a dozen calendars, some going back to the nineteen forties. There were bunches of dried flowers and herbs hanging above the fireplace and a heap of big old musty books piled on the dresser. There were ornaments everywhere - and a long row of little statues on the mantelpiece.

His grandfather had died two years ago and, since then, he had only ever come with groceries, which Nancy bought for her mother in defiance of Big Red's anger. Big Red detested Old Florrie and sometimes, when he rowed with Nancy, called her a witch, like the idiots at school. Young Red had dealt out many bloody noses in the schoolyard, but he couldn't do anything about his father.

He liked Old Florrie. She had always been kind to him; always asked after him. She had always given him sweets when he was small, or a threepenny bit or sixpence. So what if she's a witch, he thought, looking around the room. Better to be a kindly witch who helps you than a union man who makes everyone miserable.

He finished his tea and put his cup back on the tray. Old Florrie was in the kitchen; he could hear her filling the kettle. She returned to the table and sat in the opposite chair. Her movements were quick and sprightly for someone so old, but he was astonished by how much smaller she had become.

"Who comes to see you on a night, Gran? Are they criminals?" Young Red had only one direction of thought left in his head.

"No, lad. The living come for remedies and the dead, sometimes, for a bit of a chat. I see more folk now than I ever have. And more of them die every day!" She chuckled and her shadow leapt around the room. Images of Raggy flooded Young Red's mind.

"Now you bring that lamp a bit nearer and we'll see what's in the leaves."

Young Red moved the lamp and his grandmother leaned forward over his cup.

"Gran..." His voice sounded strained and desperate. "Gran, I need to know if the future's going to be okay."

The world of yellow light was behind him and he heard the back door softly close. He caught glimpses of movement in the shadows of the yard. Were they the living or the dead, he wondered, or just more idiots from the town in their hopeless disguises?

It had all been so strange. The more his grandmother had talked the more he wished he had never gone to see her. He had sat in the room of yellow light while she spoke of threads and connections and getting his life clear. He had never heard such crazy stuff in his life. He felt disappointed and confused and furious with himself. He should never have gone. Witchcraft was the resort of fools.

There might have been a little bit of him that was like Old Florrie. But only a very little bit. There was much more of him that was like his father; and that part needed hard evidence, not crazy talk, before he could understand anything. That part of him lived in the real world, where a tree was a tree, or a chair, or a stack of firewood.

His grandmother had asked him to go back for another reading after midsummer. But he wouldn't go. He didn't need anyone's help. He would work things out for himself.

By the time he had cycled home across the town Young Red's brain was spinning. He went straight to bed and lay on his back with his eyes closed. A distant drum began to pound inside his head. After a while a crashing cymbal joined in and he became too preoccupied with his physical distress to think of floating bodies or treacherous friends or strange old women who talked mumbo-jumbo.

Eventually the symptoms subsided a little and he slept. He had a frantic dream which began with him running through a tunnel. He ran and he ran but he couldn't get to the end. Someone else was there with him and he thought it might be Mouth, but he couldn't see him. Then the presence of the other person became more sinister. He ran faster and the threat became stronger still. Then the pursuing figure somehow got in front of him. He couldn't see it properly but he knew it was Raggy. He was going too fast to stop... At the moment of impact he woke up.

Chapter Eight

Saturday the thirteenth of June arrived and they had still not found Raggy's body. Shortly after her son's disappearance Freda Bottomley had gone to the police station to see if he had been arrested. The police could tell her nothing. Police Constable Mawson called at the Bottomley's house and took a few bleak details, then left to help organise a search.

But no-one knew where to look. The local paper printed an appeal for information. No-one responded. Questions were asked at the schools in the area. No pupils came forward with revelations. House to house inquiries began and petered out after a few days. Empty buildings were searched and so was the riverbank. They even went to look in the old priory and dragged the river from the bridge to the start of the weed downstream from the Blood Hole. Nothing was found. By the middle of the second week the police and their helpers had turned their attention to other more pressing business.

And Brock, Young Shack, Sally Bell and Jack Parnaby remained silent.

Every day Young Red searched the headlines as he sorted the papers into the order of his round on the counter at Ralph's shop. There was nothing in the national dailies but, at the end of the second week, when no-one had come forward with information, the local paper filled its front page with the mystery of Raggy's disappearance. The headline screamed: LOCAL YOUTH STILL MISSING and there was a fuzzy photograph of Raggy. Young Red was horrified. He rounded on Mouth accusingly.

"It was me that called for him - 'cos you were too busy going for your breakfast. What if she remembers?"

Mouth stopped sorting his papers and scowled. "Who?"

"His sister. That little Veronica."

Mouth exploded in contempt. "But she's only five and half bats! She won't remember you! She won't even know the days of the week!"

Young Red looked doubtful. "You think so?"

"Sure. Look - it's no use worrying about stuff till something happens. And if nothing happens, well... we can forget it. Okay?"

Young Red stared unhappily at the paper. He took a long time to reply. "I just think it's a shame. Raggy was all right - you know - he was a good pal in his way."

"You'll be blubbering next, you big pussy!"

"Bollocks! I just thought he was a good pal. He never fell out with any of us, did he? And he always did the shitty stuff - like being Scout."

Mouth gave Young Red a long look across the counter, but didn't say a word. When they had finished sorting their papers Mouth took a pack of cigarettes from the shelf and tossed it to Young Red. "Better give these to Belly later."

As they wheeled their bikes from the alley at the side of the shop Young Red grumbled. "That's a hundred we've taken this week! How's she get through them all? Ralph's going to miss them."

Mouth spat into the gutter. "Ralph ain't a clue what he's got or what he's sold. He never keeps no records. 'Sides, he makes enough money. A bit of pinching won't hurt him!"

"Good job he don't come down till eight. What'll we do if he gets suspicious and starts getting up early?"

"We'll find another way, okay?" Mouth cycled off across the market square to begin his paper round.

It's all right for you if things go wrong, Young Red thought. It's me that shot him. And that's what Brock will say if Belly talks.

As the days passed Young Red started to feel slightly more optimistic. Mouth had begun to think that Raggy must have floated downstream after all and somehow avoided discovery at the weirs.

"He must have gone down at night. Floated clean through when no-one was about. If he'd been here he'd have come up by now. Must have come up last week and gone through when no-one was looking. There ain't no other explanation."

"You sure?"

Mouth's face creased into a mass of puzzled furrows. "Can't see what else can have happened. But we'll keep Belly going a bit longer." He leered at Young Red. "Get her used to a good thing - and then we'll stop the cigs. When she comes begging we can do what we want with her!"

Young Red stared at his friend in dismay.

By the third Saturday in June Young Red felt buoyant enough to fancy going for a long bike ride. It was the only outdoor activity left for him to do - fishing and shooting were history. The only problem was the weather. He watched the sky all through his paper round, but the clouds grew thicker and darker. By mid-morning it was raining. Young Red knelt in the lean-to shed in the yard, cleaning the orange Carlton and waiting. By midday it was obvious that the rain was set in for the whole afternoon.

Well, he would just have to do something else. He got changed and put on his best jeans. He still didn't feel much like food, but he ate a slice of bread and jam. If he stayed in the house after one o'clock Big Red would be back from work and talk of Reeds and union power and more intelligence tests would send him blank as a zombie. He may as well go down the street and chat up a good looking bird.

It would help to take his mind off his problems and those endless thoughts about Raggy.

As he opened the door of the Espresso Coffee Bar a flood of sound from the jukebox hit Young Red and seemed to lift him up like a wave. The place was packed, which was usual on a rainy Saturday afternoon. For a few seconds he stood in the doorway as his eyes adjusted to the subdued artificial light and his ears to the thump - thump - thump of the bass drum from the jukebox. Elvis Presley was singing Jailhouse Rock and Young Red's nose wrinkled in annoyance. Why don't they change the records, he thought. That thing's ancient - they were playing it last year. He spotted Chris Marsden in the corner of the window seat and Chris waved to him to come over. Miming the action of drinking Young Red squeezed between chairs and tables to the counter and asked for an espresso.

He squeezed back across the room until he had reached the table by the window seat. He looked down at the brown curly hair and ruddy cheeks of his best cycling pal. "What's new, then?"

Chris shrugged. "Dunno. Only been here five minutes."

"Any women?"

Chris shrugged again.

"Budge up, then, and let's have a pew."

Young Red crammed himself into the twelve inch gap which appeared between Chris and a spotty fourth former called Bratt (Batty Bratty) whom he loathed. He settled his broad shoulders against the back of the plush pink cushion and stuck his elbow into Batty's ribs.

"Shove up a bit and let a man breathe, will you?" He sucked the froth from the top of his coffee and surveyed the scene before him.

Due to weekends spent adventuring with guns and bikes it had been ages since he had been to the coffee bar. During that time certain things had changed. There was a group of youths from the new council estate (he guessed, because they were strangers) crowded around a table by the door. As befitted newcomers they had the worst position in the room: in the way of people going in and out, their coffees chilled in the draught from the door. But they made the best of it, studiously ignoring the through traffic.

They evidently fancied themselves as sharp dressers. Young Red grimaced behind his cup as he eyed their tight black jeans and drape jackets, their bootlace ties and heavy crepe-soled shoes. That lot must have cost a bit. They were older than him, sixteen or seventeen, and all of them smoked ostentatiously.

In the best position - the table between the counter and the jukebox - sat the hard men from the town: Jimmy 'Ingo' Smith (nicknamed after Ingemar Johansson, soon to become world heavyweight champion) Tiny Marshall (all eighteen solid stones) Thomo, Chick-Chick and Algy Roberts, of the concrete head-butt. They sat in their black leather jackets with their armour plating of studs and their black leather gloves, all five faces below their sunglasses fixed expressionlessly on the group of strangers at the table by the door. Young Red had nothing to fear from Ingo and Tiny. They were local.

Young Red watched them and waited for the action. In a few minutes, he was sure, Algy or Chick-Chick would shuffle across the room, v-e-r-y leisurely, bend down to one of the teds by the door and inform him quietly, but finally, to tell his mates to get the hell out of there or they'd all be dead by two o'clock.

Ingo was nodding across the room at the group by the door and saying something in Chick-Chick's ear. Trouble was coming. Young Red grinned behind his coffee cup. He shifted his attention to the females, taking stock quickly, before things hotted up. The table in the far corner, traditionally the girls' table ever since the espresso bar had opened, was full of giggling fourth formers whom he saw at school every day. He felt disappointed. Nothing doing there. The same stupid chattering faces... None of them would let you touch them up. Why did they come here, he wondered, if they didn't want to screw?

He ran his gaze around the room as he sipped his espresso. Why didn't the birds from the estate come to the coffee bar? Now they would be welcome. Nothing like a pair of new tits to liven you up a bit... He wondered if Mouth would ever get a female - other than Sally Bell, who really didn't count. Mouth never came in the espresso bar. He had once tried to persuade him, but Mouth had become so wildly angry that he had backed off in alarm. Then Mouth had said that crowded places made him feel ill and he just couldn't be in them. That explained why he always made some excuse when there was a good film on at the flicks. But if he didn't go to the pictures and never went in the espresso bar how was he ever going to get a bird?

The jukebox was playing Marty Wilde's *Endless Sleep* and the words made Young Red think of Raggy floating down the river. The room drifted out of focus and his cup almost slipped from his fingers.

"For Chrissake, Chris, put something decent on that bloody machine!"

Chris shrugged. "They don't have anything decent."

"Bullshit! You're just too tight to put any money in!" Young

Red stood up. "Save my seat while I put something good on."

Young Red pushed through to the jukebox and ran his eyes over the rows of song titles. He selected Marvin Rainwater's *Whole Lotta Woman* because he still liked its odd country flavour, Eddie Cochran's *C'mon Everybody* from the 'new releases' column - and his favourite: Buddy Holly's *Peggy Sue*, with the frantic insistent drums.

"Hey, Young Red, watcha putting on?" Ingo was staring stone-faced at him across the table. Algy turned towards him and growled. "Better be fucking good, or me and Ingo gonna give you a haircut."

"It's Russ Conway, Perry Como and Connie Francis." Young Red dropped his coin into the slot and stepped back quickly as Chick-Chick made a grab for his arm.

"Better bloody not be, or we'll fucking skin you!"

The music started playing. Eddie Cochran came on first and a cheer went up from Ingo's table. Ingo gave Young Red the thumbs up and they pounded the rhythm with their fists on the table.

As he was pushing his way back to his place he heard his name called in an unfamiliar voice. He looked around and saw that one of the teds was beckoning to him from the table by the door.

"Hey, Red, c'mover here a minute. We wanna ask yuh something."

He tried to catch Ingo's eye, in order to convey a silent warning that the teds were about to make the first move, but he couldn't tell if they were aware of what was happening as their eyes were hidden behind their sunglasses. Chris was looking at him and shaking his head, mouthing to him to come back to his seat. For a moment he couldn't decide what to do.

The voice was calling again, in its odd mixture of local dialect and American hip, "Hey, man, we wanna aksya something important."

On impulse he crossed the room to the table by the door.

There were six of them, all dressed alike with long, slicked back hair, three purple drapes and three black, six pairs of black jeans, white socks, black shoes. It was either that or black leather or you were square. Young Red felt like a leftover from an antique world, in his lumberjacket and work denims.

"Hey, kid," it was a new speaker now, a blond youth with a tattoo on the back of his clenched right fist. He fixed Young Red with a lethal, ice-blue stare, leaning towards him over the table. His voice was quiet, but hard and very clear. "Hey, kid, you killed my brother. Now I'm gonna fucking kill you."

Young Red was stunned. He had expected to be given a message for Ingo, with whom the teds must have seen him talking. Instead he was being accused of something so unexpected he was unable to take it in.

"You what?" He asked stupidly.

"You killed my brother. Shot him in his back, you fucking red-haired bastard. Now I'm gonna cut yuh to fucking pieces."

The eyes remained fixed on Young Red's face, pinning him to the spot with their intent.

"You with red hair and two of your fucking mates shot him down the river. Admit it now, and I'll only kill yuh once."

Young Red swallowed, his mind a racing blank. He opened his mouth with the idea of denying the accusation and said, to his utter astonishment, in the sudden silence between Eddie Cochran and Marvin Rainwater, "You piss off back to where you belong, or you'll be dead and buried in less time than it takes me to spit!"

Things happened so quickly Young Red was never certain afterwards of the precise order of events. He remembered the blond youth making a rapid movement with his tattooed hand and he saw that the tattoo was a bird - a swallow, he thought. Then the swallow flew towards his head. He saw the knife too late and felt something happen to the left side of his face. Then he was pulled backwards by a pair of powerful hands and dumped into the lap of a fourth year on the girls' table. The girl, who was called Angela Dixon, was already screaming. Bodies were rushing past him and voices were yelling. He felt a cool draught on his face and thought the door must be open and that everyone was running out and leaving him to be killed. Then he heard Angela's voice screaming, "Blood! Blood! Look at the blood!" He looked down and saw that his shirt was wet through with blood. He thought that he must be going to die and was surprised it was so painless. Then Chris appeared above him and grabbed his arm and pulled him to his feet and dragged him out of the door into the street. He caught two distinct images as he started to run, Chris still pulling on his arm: the first was of the blond youth lying on the pavement and the second was of two policemen running neck and neck like sprinters up the middle of the street.

"Man, you were brilliant! You were one-hundred-per-cent totally brilliant!" Chris hovered excitedly around Young Red, his ruddy cheeks glowing like fires, as Janet dabbed at her brother's face with cotton wool, which she kept dipping into a bowl of crimson water on the dining room table.

The sight of the water discoloured with his own blood made Young Red feel light-headed. He had a hollow feeling in his chest and he wondered if he was going to faint, but the stinging in his cheek when Janet dabbed it brought him back to full painful consciousness.

"It's a good job it was me what was in and not Mam and Dad. They'd have gone crackers seeing you come in with blood down to your waist!"

"Where've they gone?" Young Red still felt shaken, but was enjoying the attentions of his ministering sister.

"Got a message soon after you went out. Gran's had a fall, or something, and they've gone to see to her. Dad didn't want to - and he grumbled like hell - 'cos he'd just come in and wanted a bath, but he went in case she needed lifting."

Chris was sitting at the table, grinning at Young Red as if he had won an Olympic medal.

"You should have seen him, Jan. He stood up to the whole table full of them and told this ted where he could shove himself! Then this ted swiped at him with his flick-knife and Algy pulled him away and Tiny and Thomo and them was beating hell out of them and Ingo got hold of this ted with the knife and broke his arm and chucked him into the street and kicked him and then someone shouts ayup it's the law and Ingo and them ran off down White Horse passage and we came here sharpish."

"I hope the police didn't recognise your hair. You'll have to dye it, like mine." Janet laughed and tossed back her glossy brown curls. "Mind you, it costs a bit to have it done right."

Young Red became testy. "Don't want to dye my hair! I ain't done nothing wrong! It was them that started it!"

"What did they pick on you for, then? You must have done something. They wouldn't have started on you for nothing with Ingo and them in there."

"I didn't do nothing." Young Red avoided his sister's eyes. "Must have thought I was someone else."

"Pull the other one, Ronnie, it's got bells on!" Janet shook her head. "One of these days you'll get in too deep with that Len Dykes and no-one'll be able to help you! There. That's the best I can do. You should go to hospital and have them look at it - but I suppose the police'll be checking there."

She dried his face with a clean piece of cotton wool. Young Red stood up and went to look at himself in the long mirror above the mantelpiece. A thin red line about two inches long ran across his left cheekbone.

"Don't look like much." He ran his finger warily along the line. "Hurts a bit, but not a lot. How long will it take to go?"

Janet came and stood beside him. They looked solemnly at each other in the mirror.

"It'll show up for a few weeks yet. You'll mebbe have a small mark there for ever."

Young Red studied the reflection of his new face.

"I might get a different name now. Scarface. Like in the film." He grinned boldly around the room from the mirror. Janet turned away to clear the mess from the table.

"Bad enough having red hair. With a scar as well you won't get away with anything."

"Shit! I hadn't thought of that!" Young Red glared at the face in the mirror, as if it was his worst enemy. He had a sudden urge to get out of the house before his parents returned and started asking awkward questions.

"Tell Mam and Dad I had a fall from my bike."

Perhaps the scar would have gone by the time he got back.

Young Red had tea at Chris Marsden's and they went for a short bike ride in the evening, as the weather had begun to clear. During the ride Chris prattled about the fight in the espresso bar. Such incidents were new to him, but they were becoming commonplace to Young Red, after months of close association with Mouth. Young Red ignored his excited companion and kept looking at his watch.

"What's up, Red?" Chris eventually asked. "You got a date?"

"Have to get back soon. Want to see if my gran's all right." It was only half the truth, but enough to convince Chris.

"Christ, I hope she is, Red. Must be as bad as getting beat up having a fall when you're that old."

Young Red winced. Better not to speak, he thought. People always said stuff you didn't want to hear.

He was back in the yard by ten, before the pubs closed and the second house at the cinema finished. His bravado of the afternoon had gradually evaporated, leaving him with a sinking feeling of foreboding. He was sure he had been recognised running away from the coffee bar and that the whole town was muttering about him from the shadows. When he arrived home he expected Mawson to be sitting in the front room with his notebook open on the drop-leaf table.

But he knew he hadn't killed the blond ted's brother. It would have been in the paper and the gossip of the town if the kid had died. Even Raggy - from just about the poorest family in the town - had been the subject on everyone's lips for the best part of a week...

To his surprise his father greeted him like the prodigal son.

"So here's the flying cyclist! You'd best be getting a crash helmet for a machine as dangerous as that! You want to watch they don't nab you for speeding or for flying without a licence!"

He couldn't think of anything to say in response to his father's joviality. It was so unexpected he waited for the hidden trap. Big Red's jokes had been, all too often, the last gleam of light before

87

a storm. He noticed his jacket and shirt hanging on the drying rack above the hearth. He turned his back on them and stared at the blank TV screen, feeling awkward.

"How's Gran?"

"She's as tough as a tanner's boot is your gran." Big Red's features clouded briefly. "There's some who'd say more's the pity... When Mary Lythe came running in here I thought, way she were talking, that she'd dropped down dead in her yard. But when we gets there she's sitting in her front room drinking a cup of tea! Mary were as amazed as us to see she had recovered so quick." His humour returned as he eyed Young Red's self-conscious face. "Looks like our Janet's done a fair job on your head. Pity she can't see her way to washing a teacup once in a while!"

Nancy appeared in the doorway with a clean tablecloth and removed the old one, which was speckled with blood from the afternoon. Young Red tried to catch his mother's attention. He would get more detail from her.

"Jan said something about Gran having a fall."

His mother smoothed out the new tablecloth. "We think your gran had a mild heart attack. We wanted her to go to hospital, but she wouldn't go. She said she'd be all right once she knew you were safe."

Nancy straightened the edges of the tablecloth. Big Red stared resolutely at the floor.

"Me?" Young Red looked from his mother to his father, wondering what could be coming next. His mother began setting the table for supper. Big Red cleared his throat and ran his fingers through his thinning hair.

"Seems your gran had some crazy idea that a bird had flown into your face. I told her no matter how fast you was going on your bike a bird weren't likely to be slow enough to hit you." He ended irritably. "I think she's off her head, but your mother, of course, don't agree."

Young Red sat down heavily at the table. The world had become too much for him; its extremes were too wide for him to bridge. It was a world where birds suddenly became knives and friends became enemies; a world where ordinary places were suddenly full of danger. It was a world where strange old women knew stuff that was happening when they weren't there... Young Red put his fingers to the scar on his cheek. There must be something in witchcraft after all.

"You all right, Ronnie?" His mother was looking at him keenly across the table. Her eyes reminded him of his own. She was Old Florrie's daughter. He was Nancy's son. "It wasn't a bird that flew at you, was it?"

"No..." Young Red managed to gasp.

"No - not really. I just weren't watching where I was going, that's all."

He woke from a troubled sleep. There was a dim light in the room which filtered through his curtains from the new orange streetlamps they had put up a few months earlier. He turned on to his side and saw Raggy sitting in the basket chair that stood by his bedroom window. He was dripping wet and his face was half covered with riverweed. Young Red stared at the figure, paralysed, as an icy sweat formed on his face. Summoning all his will he leapt out of bed, with the intention of pitching both the chair and its gruesome occupant out of the window.

"Gerraway!" He roared. "Gerrawaaaaay!"

The chair was empty. On the seat were the clothes he had taken off earlier, dry as new biscuits.

He stumbled out of his room on to the landing, feeling dizzy and shaken. His mother met him at the top of the stairs in her dressing gown.

"What is it, Ronnie? What were you shouting for?"

"He was there! There! I saw him!" His voice was strained with shock and fear.

"Who, Ronnie - who?" His mother took hold of his arm and he realised he was trembling. He pulled away and lurched into the bathroom.

"No-one." He called over his shoulder. "It was a... a dream."

"You can't go round shouting in the middle of the night, Ronnie. You've woke us all up!" His mother accused him through the bathroom door. "If you have bad dreams you'll have to sleep downstairs!"

As he washed his face he knew Raggy was everywhere. Dead but everywhere. Around every corner. Hidden in the outlines of the night. Waiting. It was only a matter of time before he drove him crazy.

From that moment he slept with the light on.

CHAPTER NINE

Sunday was fine so Young Red cycled out to the castle. It was a round trip of twenty miles and the exercise and fresh air made him feel less oppressed. Cycling was the only time when he didn't feel trapped; it was the only time he could escape his problems, escape from himself. He went alone, as company drew him back to the nightmare web of his life.

As he rode he wondered why Old Florrie hadn't given him some kind of warning about what was going to happen. She had obviously seen something, because she had known about the bird... Why wouldn't she tell him the truth? Did she think it would be more than he could cope with? She had gone on about his connections - about stuff he didn't understand. Why hadn't she just told him to watch out when he went into the town? Young Red felt exposed to a world of dangers that lurked just beyond the range of his eyes.

It dawned on him that this was Old Florrie's world: the world that she could reach through her witchcraft. A world where a tree was a tree until it fell on you. Where a swallow was a bird until it became a knife. Then he realised it wouldn't have made any difference if she had warned him. Things came at you so fast you only remembered warnings afterwards, when it was too late. In that case what use was witchcraft?

You may as well live in the world as you saw it. And if a bird became a knife with luck it might only brush against your cheek.

He lay on the grass in the sun for an hour at the castle, staring at the sky and the top of the Norman keep. A family was picnicking on the grass beneath the bailey wall and a man was throwing a stick for his dog. It was a peaceful scene. But, as he lay watching, he felt an undertow of darkness, as if they were all sliding towards the edge of a cliff - that somehow it was only the picnicking and the stick throwing that was keeping them from going over. In his own case, he realised, it was cycling.

As long as I'm on my bike I'll be all right, he thought. As long as I'm moving. Then nothing can get to you. But you had to get off sometime. And that was when the trouble began.

He rode back to town feeling almost calm. When he got home he found Police Constable Mawson sitting in the front room with his notebook open on the drop-leaf table.

Mawson stood up and eyed Young Red as if he was something that should have been poisoned by the council pest controller. He looked at everyone that way, unless they had higher rank. He addressed the woman who hovered in the doorway in a dry, sterile voice.

"I would like a word with your son alone, Mrs Patterson, if you have no objection."

"Oh, but I do object!" Nancy stuck her chin out stubbornly. "And I want my husband in here too." She turned towards the dining room. "Red! Come in and see what the policeman has to say."

Big Red ambled into the sitting room. He looked Mawson up and down as if he was a new apprentice on his first morning at Reeds.

"Now then, mister, let's be getting on with it. We're busy folks round here and haven't much time for gassing." Big Red's tone was sombre and his heavy gaze settled on the policeman like an invisible weight. Mawson continued, his expressionless voice unchanged.

"Could we be seated? What I have to say will take some time."

"Be seated if you like."

Big Red sat in an armchair in front of the empty grate. His hostile eyes never left the policeman.

"Sit down, Ronnie." Nancy perched on the edge of a straight-backed chair near the door. Young Red flopped into the only other armchair which faced the window. Mawson resumed his seat at the table and glanced down at his notebook.

"You are Ronald Patterson?"

"Yep." Young Red stared sullenly at the window.

"You live at this address?" Mawson read the address from his notebook.

"Yep."

In spite of his anxiety Young Red was assailed by the image of Mawson in his pacamac, in the corner of Ginner Lund's field.

"Were you at the Espresso Coffee Bar on the afternoon of Saturday the twentieth of June?"

Young Red made no reply so Mawson rephrased the question.

"Were you there yesterday afternoon?"

"Yep."

Young Red shifted slightly and frowned. He dare not tell an outright lie. His presence could have been mentioned by any number of people. He thought of Mawson in the field: up and down, up and down; creak-creak, creak-creak, screwing some tart from a bar out of town.

"There was a disturbance about one forty-five. What can you tell me about it?"

Young Red shuffled his feet and looked down at the carpet.

"Nothing."

The image of Mawson in the field was replaced by a flying swallow.

"But you were there and there was a fight? One person is still in hospital in a critical condition." Mawson added, with an icy smirk. "He may die."

What's another death? Young Red thought. Hope it's the moron with the knife.

"How did it start?"

"Dunno. Couldn't see."

"So you admit there was a fight?"

"Dunno. Couldn't see." Young Red stared at the window.

"How did you get that scar on your left cheek?"

Young Red flinched. The image of the swallow flew into the side of his head.

"Fell... fell off my bike."

"When?"

"Yesterday."

"How?"

Young Red couldn't think.

"Weren't..." he clasped and unclasped his hands, "weren't looking where I was going."

Mawson sat up very straight and alert.

"But you said you were in the coffee bar yesterday."

"I fell... afterwards." Young Red's gaze was back on the carpet. His hands were tightly clasped.

"Where did you fall from your bike?"

Young Red went blank. An idea rushed into his mind.

"Dunno. Hit my head on something... Can't remember."

"How did you get home?"

"Dunno. Can't remember."

"You didn't fall on a flick-knife, by any chance?"

It's him, Young Red thought. He's going to die.

"I said I fell off my bike."

A fixed frosty smile had appeared on Mawson's face.

"But we have witnesses. You have been identified. You started a fight in the coffee bar..."

"I didn't do nothing! I fell! I told you!" Young Red glared at the policeman; his face was redder than his hair. Mawson continued as if he had not been interrupted.

"In the coffee bar yesterday. You attacked one Andrew Clowes, who is at present in hospital and, if he dies, you will be guilty of ..."

"Eyup, there, mister - you're overstepping the mark!" Big Red had risen from his chair. "We've heard enough of your mealy-mouthed nonsense! It's time you was on your way!"

Mawson stood up too. He picked up his notebook and put it in his pocket. The frosty smile had gone.

"I'll be back." His sterile tone was unaltered. "I'll let myself out."

No-one moved until the front door had closed. Young Red was distraught. He couldn't accuse the ted of attacking him because then he would have to confess to the hunt by the river and then they would go and question Mouth and Brock and then Brock would tell about Raggy and then he would go to gaol anyway - so he may as well go now for something he hadn't done, rather than go later for something that was worse... He might only get a couple of years, he thought, for attacking the ted with the knife. How long he would get for shooting Raggy, who had been completely unarmed, he couldn't bring himself to imagine.

Nancy looked at her son, her face crumpled with concern.

"Was any of that true, Ronnie? Did you start a fight in the coffee bar?" She lost control. "It's that Leonard Dykes! He's made you into a criminal like himself!"

Big Red silenced her outburst with a leaden stare.

"If he did start a fight, and that Andrew lad dies, he'd better have a good tale for yon bobby!" He lowered his voice to a growl. "He means to get you, lad. And there's not much more I can do to stop him!"

Young Red got slowly to his feet.

"There was a fight." He stated flatly. "But I never hit anyone. It were someone else."

"Why didn't you tell him, Ronnie? Then he'll leave you alone. I'll tell him!" Nancy rushed towards the door. "I'll shout him back and you can tell him!"

"No!" The urgency in Young Red's voice stopped his mother in the doorway.

"But, Ronnie..." she pleaded, confused, "if you didn't do anything..."

"No. I don't tell on folks. Telling's the worst thing anyone can do in their whole lives. It's worse than..." Young Red couldn't think of a comparison to describe so unspeakable a crime. "Worse than anything."

Big Red nodded approvingly at his son. Solidarity was something he could understand.

"If you're going to stick together, lad, just make sure you're on the side what's going to win."

They came for him the next morning after he had got back from his paper round. He was in the middle of his breakfast and he had to go without his toast and marmalade. Two uniformed officers he didn't recognise came for him in a patrol car. His father and sister had gone to work and it was his mother who had to endure his departure alone. Nancy didn't cry, but she grabbed his hands as they told him he was being arrested for the assault on Andrew Clowes and she squeezed them hard for a moment before they put the handcuffs on. He couldn't remember what she had been saying to him as he left.

He did his best to try to keep calm. He was sitting on the back seat handcuffed to one of the officers and, as he rode along, he clenched his fists to stop his hands from shaking. The effort caused the muscles of his forearms to go into spasm and the constable next to him told him to keep still, as the uncontrollable jerking of his elbows dug the officer in the ribs.

They led him into a large room with a sort of counter and removed the handcuffs. The constable with the handcuffs winked at his companion as he fastened them on to his belt. After he had given a third officer behind the counter his name and address and date of birth he was taken along a corridor into another room where they took his finger prints. Then he was moved again and left by himself in a small room with no windows. It was warm in the room but he began to shiver. The only furniture was a table and two wooden chairs. He sat on one of the chairs and hugged his knees to stop his legs from trembling. He sat like that for what seemed like hours. Eventually he began to think he had been forgotten. Perhaps they had arrested Ingo and would be letting him go home... He relaxed a little and the shivering stopped.

He became hungry and thirsty by turn. The hunger went off after a while, but his mouth and tongue became as dry as ashes. The lights were bright and the air was stuffy and his head started to ache. There was no clock in the room and they had taken his watch away from him at the counter. At some point in the timeless brightness the door opened and, almost with a sense of relief, he realised he had been remembered.

A different officer questioned him. There was no sign of Mawson. Maybe they've given him the sack, Young Red thought, because he's no good at asking questions. The new officer went on and on about the fight in the coffee bar, but he had no more talent for the job than Mawson.

"But you were in the coffee bar and your friends were there with you. James Smith was there, wasn't he?"

The policeman approached Young Red and stood looking down at him. Young Red sat on his chair and stared past the policeman at the corner of the ceiling.

"It was James Smith who suggested you pick a fight with Andrew Clowes, wasn't it? The policeman yelled at Young Red, "Wasn't it, you lying bastard?"

"No." Young Red continued to stare at the corner of the ceiling. The next thing he knew he was sprawling on his back on the floor and his head was ringing, like the time his father slapped him for being an hour late for tea.

He stood up groggily and looked around the room. He felt shocked and angry. His chair lay on its side in the corner. The wooden frame of the back had split away from the seat. The policeman was also staring at the chair. With a curse the policeman picked up the broken chair and, without a glance or a word to Young Red, carried it out of the room.

Young Red's anger slowly subsided. He sat on the only remaining chair and held his head in his hands until the ringing decreased and was replaced by a dull throbbing. In spite of the pain he was filled with a profound sense of triumph. The police knew nothing about the business with Raggy... He couldn't care less what they did about the fight with Andrew Clowes. Andrew Clowes was nothing. Just a greasy ted from the estate.

Eventually his feeling of triumph faded and he was left with his headache. He rested his head on his folded arms on the table and was trying to think of Sally Bell when the door opened again and his name was called from the corridor. He followed yet another officer into a different room where he was told to sit down and was given a cup of tea. The officer left the room.

"Now then. That's better. Nothing like a cup of tea when times are rough, don't you think?" The voice was well spoken and friendly, with no trace of the local accent. Young Red squinted over the top of his cup at the speaker, a chubby, round faced man, in a suit and tie, smiling at him from behind a desk. The smile seemed different from the usual smiles of police: the mouth and eyes both smiled at the same time. Young Red stared at the chubby man.

"Drink up, that's a good chap. Do you want something to eat? A sandwich, perhaps? Or a sausage roll?" The chubby man's eyebrows went up and down in time with his questions. He reminded Young Red of a clown. Young Red shook his head and the chubby man seemed disappointed.

"As you wish. But I recommend the cheese and tomato sandwiches if you change your mind." The man pulled his chair up to the desk, took a fountain pen from his jacket pocket and removed the top with a flourish. Young Red watched over the rim of his cup, which he held in front of his face with both hands. The man produced a sheet of white paper from a drawer in the desk and began to write on it. The pen squeaked like an irritated insect as it moved over the paper. The man stopped writing suddenly and looked up.

"Most unfortunate business, that rumpus in the coffee bar - don't you think? Bad characters, those louts from the estate. Simply asking for trouble, coming down into the town and shoving their noses in where they're not wanted - don't you agree?" The chubby faced man's eyebrows went up and down.

"Enough to make anyone really angry. Troublemakers. Coming down just to cause trouble - right?"

Young Red stared woodenly over his cup and said nothing.

"All a self-respecting chap could do. I mean, coming down like that and shoving their noses in. Trying to get off with the birds. All a chap could do. Tell them to beat it. To get back where they belong - right?"

Young Red sipped his tea and stared in silence at the round faced man.

"Course they wouldn't go. And that was really stupid. Just shows how stupid those louts from the estate are, doesn't it? Nothing for it but to get them out yourself. You and your mates. Couldn't lose face in front of the birds, hey? Couldn't look like a wetneck in front of the women." The man in the suit smiled sympathetically at Young Red. "I understand. I'd have done the same thing myself. More tea?"

Young Red didn't speak. He stared at the man unblinkingly over his cup. The round faced man sighed.

"Well, that's how it was. Quite natural. Quite understandable." He smiled at Young Red. "Well, now that we know what happened we can get the business sorted out and you can go home." He shifted the paper on his desk. "I just want to jot down the main facts and we can call it a day." He held his fountain pen to the sheet of paper and smiled encouragingly.

"You arrived at the coffee bar at half past one. That's about right - wouldn't you say?"

Young Red put his empty cup down on the edge of the desk.

"Get stuffed. You can just jot that down on your stupid piece of paper."

This time they locked him in the cells. But he didn't care - didn't mind what they did to him. He knew he had beaten them - that they couldn't make him talk. He hadn't let Ingo down. His father's words replayed themselves, "If you're going to stick together, just make sure you're on the side what's going to win." Young Red saw again his father's glance of encouragement. He felt suddenly closer to Big Red and despised Brock utterly. What kind of turd could be your friend one day and, when it suited him, your enemy the next? He walked up and down between the sleeping shelf and the toilet, flexing his shoulders, trying to work himself into a state of readiness in case they decided to come in and really beat him up. From the tales Mouth had told him beatings in police cells were commonplace.

He walked up and down for a while and then sat on the sleeping shelf. Gradually he was invaded by a dreadful sense of emptiness. Was this what his life was going to be like from now on: dragged in for questioning whenever an incident occurred in the town? Mouth had said that was what happened once the bobbies got their knives into you... It's all right for them, Young Red thought, the law lets them stab you as often as they want.

Little by little his father resumed his authoritarian remoteness; the unexpected fellowship he had felt between them faded away. And, inexorably, his fear of Brock returned.

He sat there in his newfound emptiness until they came for him and took him to the reception desk. The duty officer handed him back his belongings: an old Ingersoll watch, a clasp-knife, a few coins. He had to sign to say he had received them and, because of the emptiness, it took him a long time to remember his name.

Young Red stood on the pavement outside the police station in a strangely familiar town. It was as if he had been away for years. He set off slowly along the street wondering, after so long away, what he was supposed to do now he had returned.

It was still quite light. He didn't want to go home. Home meant more voices, more questions - he'd had voices and questions all day. He walked in his emptiness without direction or purpose. As he walked he was aware of a new sadness that he hadn't noticed before. The sadness was in the streets, the people, himself, everything. There was an absence of meaning too in the sadness - it was just there because it was there, like a sooty roof or a streetlamp. The wind and the sky were full of sadness - sadness was what the world was made of. The church clock struck eight and he paused to listen as the sound wafted over the town. The solemn strokes of the clock seemed, to Young Red, like the tones of a funeral bell. Raggy has beaten us all, he thought. He has escaped and has no more pointless pain to bear. Raggy was lucky.

An idea was beginning to filter into his mind. He walked down a couple more streets, turned a corner and went into a fish and chip shop. Ingo's mother, lardy and plain in her greasy apron, was behind the counter wrapping up the orders. A square, scowling man in a white coat was frying fish.

Young Red joined the queue, catching the woman's eye quite unintentionally. She looked troubled and signalled for him to go through a half door in the counter.

"Wait in the passage, love. I'll be with you in a minute."

He stood in a tiled passage with greasy mops and buckets of chips and trays of fish. Ingo's mother came in, a little breathless, clutching a paper parcel.

"Oo, love, are you all right? What did them bloody coppers do to you?" Her tone was solicitous and warm.

"Not a lot." He looked down at her gloomily. Must be all over town by now, he thought: Young Red the troublemaker, carted off to the station again. "I just came to ask you to tell Ingo I never told."

"Oo, you're the best lad in town, Ronnie Patterson. I wish you were mine." Ingo's mother gushed at him. "Here..." She thrust the paper parcel into his hands. "I wish I could do more, love, but..."

"It's all right. Just tell Ingo." A thought leaped into his brain. "That lad in hospital - didn't die did he?"

Ingo's mother looked aghast.

"Why no, love! Peggy Marshall works at the hospital and she was in here half an hour since. Told me that lad had no more'n a busted jaw and a big bruise on his bum!"

Young Red sat on a seat by the war memorial at the farthest end of the main street from the river and unwrapped the fish and chips Ingo's mother had given him. He ate a few chips and half the fish and gave the rest to a stray dog that had been watching him hungrily from a safe distance. The animal had a ring of fur missing from around its neck from being constantly tethered. Young Red watched it gobble the fish and chips. Must have broken free, he thought. Good luck to it. The dog loped off with its tail down and never looked back; he watched it until it disappeared around a corner.

An evening wind sprang up, sending his chip wrappers skittering across the street into the doorway of a boarded up shop. After a while a tramp with a paper sack came and sat on the other end of the seat. The tramp nodded at Young Red.

"Nice night."

Irish, Young Red thought. A roadster.

"Not bad. Going far?"

"Shrewsbury today. Newcastle tomorrow. Give us a tanner."

Young Red gave him a threepenny bit.

"A blessing on you, me boy!" The tramp grinned toothlessly at him and coughed.

"Thanks." Young Red smiled vacantly back.

"It'll buy me a mug of tea, will this. And that mug of tea'll get me to York."

Young Red stared at the tramp in amazement.

The church clock struck nine and Young Red left the tramp to stretch out on the seat, his head on his paper sack. He trudged wearily home. He needed a good night's ghost-free sleep. Tomorrow would be another glorious day.

Chapter Ten

Ralph Parnaby had two other paper boys who shared responsibility for the morning deliveries with Mouth and Young Red. The river was the demarcation line between rounds, Graham Dill and Stephen Dale delivering south of the bridge, Young Red and Mouth to the north. In early July Graham Dill sprained his ankle and Ralph divided his round and his pay between Stephen Dale and Young Red. The extra money was useful and Young Red felt obliged to accept. He wanted to appear helpful and willing, because the daily theft of cigarettes had become another source of anxiety. He wanted to appear to Ralph to be above suspicion.

Mouth and Young Red always arrived at the shop early and had almost always gone before the others arrived. Odd times they would spot the two younger youths crossing the market square as they wheeled their laden bikes out of Ralph's alley. At these times Mouth would invariably break out into the rhyming couplets he reserved for the objects of his derision, "Hey, Dilly Dally, don't shilly-shally," and "Ralph's sharpened his axe and he's gone doo-lally, you're going to get the chop and he's waiting in the alley!" Mouth would laugh as they watched them hurrying towards the shop. "There go a couple of willing slaves. If you told them black was white they'd be that scared they'd agree with you!"

With half of Dilly's round to do as well as his own Young Red arrived at the shop even earlier than usual, so that he and Mouth could still leave together. The routine had developed where Mouth always took the cigarettes from the shelves behind the counter, while Young Red kept lookout by the door. Then Mouth would give the packs to him and he would put them into the deep inside pockets of his lumberjacket. Young Red felt disinclined to change things, as he was always the one who carried the cigarettes to school and therefore it was he who gave Sally Bell her share and, over the weeks, they had formed a kind of bond which he didn't want Mouth to break. He wanted to make sure Sally Bell kept quiet about their row that day in the Swamp - and Mouth had a habit of upsetting people, no matter how much you tried to limit his influence. He knew if Mouth gave Sally Bell the cigarettes pretty soon he would be taunting her and they'd be fighting. Then Sally Bell would tell what she had overheard - and neither of them knew just how much that was.

Young Red decided to do his extra half-round first, to get it out of the way, so he set off through the town towards the bridge just before seven. It was the first time he had crossed the river since the night he had found the drowned sheep. A feeling of unreality gripped him as he caught sight of the water. He dismounted and stared at the swirling current, as a hostage might look at the barrel of his captor's gun. Then he wished he hadn't, because he could see the thing lying on the bank.

It was only a boot. A simple black wellington boot. But Young Red was in no doubt about its owner.

How long it had been lying there he couldn't guess, on a little crescent of mud a few yards upriver from the southern end of the bridge. It was the splashes of green paint on the side of the boot that revealed its origins - he had noticed them on the day of the flood, when they had stopped to let Brock dry his socks. The splashes of gloss paint had kept catching his eye every time he looked at Raggy afterwards.

Young Red had never experienced anything akin to the feelings that beset him as he stared down from the bridge. If Raggy had been lying there instead of just his boot he couldn't imagine feeling worse. He had to get rid of the boot. He had to. Not because it would be recognised by anyone else (Ma Bottoms-up probably wouldn't know if Raggy even owned a pair of wellingtons) but because of what it was. It was his. It reminded Young Red of the worst moments of his life.

He glanced around; there was no-one about. Leaning his bike against the wall at the end of the bridge he was about to leap over the stile when a cheerful voice hailed him.

"Now then, Young Red. Don't see you down here this early. Going fishing tonight?"

Young Red wheeled around like a cornered animal. It was Tommy Page the postman, the town's master pike fisherman. Where in hell had he sprung from?

"Now, Tommy. Just taking a quick look at the river. Thought I might do a spot of pikeing at the Blood Hole sometime." Lying had become a way of life.

Tommy had stopped, but he didn't get off his post-bike. Young Red noticed the full postbags and realised he had just started his round.

"I'll be down here myself by six. You come down about then, Young Red, afore the rest gets here. We'll give them old pike something to think about, eh?"

Tommy rode away. But there was a bloke in a boiler suit now walking towards the northern end of the bridge and a couple of fellows in donkey jackets further up the street. Young Red cursed and rode off to start his round. On his way back across the bridge half an hour later he passed Mawson cycling the other way. The policeman glared and started to slow down, but Young Red pedalled furiously up the hill and, looking back, saw that Mawson had gone. But it was too late now. Too busy. He would have to come back tonight.

He waited for Mouth who had to pass the end of his street and they cycled slowly to school together.

"Saw Raggy's boot by the bridge this morning," Young Red had decided he needed an accomplice.

"Shit!"

Mouth spat at a passing third year. "How d'you know it were Raggy's boot?"

"It had green paint all over it."

Mouth nodded. He had noticed the paint too.

"I have to get rid of it."

"No you ain't! No-one'll know whose boot it is."

"I have to! I'd have done it this morning if it hadn't been for bloody Tommy Page. Will you keep a lookout?"

"Why not?" Mouth grinned, "if it'll stop you going nuts."

"What d'you mean?" Young Red slowed the Carlton, "who's going nuts?"

"It's just what I've seen." Mouth looked at his friend with concern, but he couldn't prevent the ghost of a mocking sneer from stealing across his features. "You're always muttering to yourself and looking about and fiddling with your hair and trying to flatten it down and putting your hand over that cut on your face. It's obvious. You're going potty!"

Young Red stared at Mouth, too dumbfounded to say a word.

It was almost dark. The occasion reminded Young Red of the time he had gone to look for Raggy's body by the landing stages. He recalled again the alien landscape of willows and water and how he had been reassured by the evidence of man's presence: the lights of the town and the solid feel of the gaff-hook in his hand. The natural world was too big without something to hang on to. It wiped away the idea you had of yourself like a rotten tree in a flood.

"You going down, or not? I can't stand here all night," Mouth scowled. He hadn't really wanted to come. "May's well have a flashing light on my head to tell the whole town what we're doing."

"Okay."

Young Red climbed over the stile and lowered himself carefully down the steep bank towards the water. He reached the crescent of mud and looked about for the boot.

"What the hell you doing?" Mouth's urgent whisper came from above. "Kick it in the fucking water and let's go!"

"Can't find it," Young Red called up, "you come down and help me look."

"Shit!" Mouth was at his side in a moment. "You're bloody useless! You'll get us both locked up! Where the hell'd you see it?"

"Just here. On the mud."

Mouth bent down, peering into the water and up and down the bank.

"Well it ain't here. It's either got washed away and sunk, or you're seeing things."

"It was here! I saw it as plain as I see you now!"

"Well it ain't here, is it?" Mouth snapped angrily at his troubled friend. "If it was here it's gone. Let's get out of this bloody creepy place!"

He disappeared up the bank. Reluctantly, Young Red followed him.

On his way across the bridge the next morning Young Red looked down at the scene of their futile search, half hoping, half dreading to see the boot they had somehow missed. But the crescent of mud was empty, except for four deep impressions where they had stood the night before. Young Red stared at the empty mud. The boot had been there... Hadn't it?

He was going mad. If Mouth said so it must be true. Mouth had a way of seeing straight into folks and he was usually right. His mind was playing tricks now, imagining things that didn't exist. There was nothing he could do to stop it - he was as good as locked up in a loony-bin already. But perhaps it would be better than going to gaol.

He started visiting the Swamp with Sally Bell at lunchtimes. They smoked the stolen cigarettes and listened to music on her radio. He needed the cigarettes - and the music. Especially the rock and roll. For a little while he could float among soft pillows of smoke in a torment-free world of drums and guitars.

Sometimes he touched Sally Bell's breasts under her jumper. And that made him forget about everything.

But there were times when his fears gripped him too tight for escape.

"Do you think I'm crazy, Sal?" he asked one day as they lay side by side smoking.

"Most folks seem crazy to me, Red. There's that many things folk have to put up with it's no wonder." She turned the dial on her radio, scanning the music stations. "Everything's so boring. Winter's boring. School's boring. This town's boring. There's no life anywhere. If it weren't for the summer and all the new music I'd be crazy too."

"I don't mean that kind of crazy, Sal. I mean really crazy. Like seeing stuff that ain't there. Like stuff you only think's there, but isn't really real." He frowned. He wasn't explaining himself at all well. Sally Bell kept distracting him, fiddling with the radio.

Sally Bell laughed. "I see Young Red every time I wake up and afore I go to sleep, but he ain't as real as he could be! Come down to the priory tonight, Red. We can do what we like - there won't be anyone round."

"Can't. Not tonight. But I will - soon."

"When's soon?"

"Soon. Maybe Saturday."

"Promise?"

"Okay," Young Red was hardly aware of what he was saying. Other thoughts and ideas were crowding into his mind. "I promise."

He left her some cigarettes and went to the cloakroom to wet his hair. The water made it look darker for a time and he felt, for a little while, less conspicuous.

Young Red stood in the shaft of yellow light while Old Florrie struggled with the chain on the back door.

"You said to come back after midsummer, Gran. Well, it's July now." He added lamely, "so I thought I'd come."

They drank tea in the room of yellow light and shadow. Their silence became so profound his own voice startled him.

"I've had a lot of trouble since I came to see you afore, Gran." He hesitated. "I was wondering if I was going to have more of it in the future."

Old Florrie's face was in shadow; Young Red couldn't see her eyes, but he felt they were fixed on his own.

"That's life, lad. Trouble's all we have. You've got to be faster than light to get the other side of it."

"But..." Young Red began to protest, "how can I do that, Gran? How can a person be as fast as that? Things come at you that quick I don't know what's happened till it's over."

"You have to cut your connections, lad. You can be like the wind then. Like the sun. Like the night. Like anything you want."

Young Red shook his head, "I don't understand."

"It's hard, lad. But it's your connections that slow you down.

They bind you that tight you're like a person head to foot in bandages."

"What connections, Gran?"

"Whatever ties you. Whatever stops your life. You're like a fly in a spider's web, lad. You need to cut through the threads."

Young Red made an effort to gather his jumbled wits.

"What threads, Gran? Which ones do I need to cut?"

"All of them, lad. You've a hard road and a lot of cutting to do."

"But I don't understand what you mean, Gran. It's too difficult... I can't..." he was lost for words, "I can't understand."

"Cut the threads, lad. Get clear of your life and you'll get your life clear. You'll understand what I'm telling you soon enough."

"But, gran..."

Old Florrie cut him off.

"That's all I can tell you. Come back again if you want. Now you'll have to go. There'll be others waiting."

He left through the haunted yard. He was so overcome with confusion he almost forgot his bike. I must have been mad to go back there, he thought as he cycled home. But I am mad, so I went. The only thing to do was to forget about witchcraft and strange old women and get on with some serious cycling. That was the thing. Get out on the open road. Get moving.

But he knew, as these thoughts passed through his head, that his life was set in concrete and, try as he might, he could not escape a single moment's pain.

All the following weekend Young Red worked fanatically on the Carlton; he had to keep busy, to block the terror of his growing madness. He stripped the bike down to no more than wheels and frame and took great pleasure in demonstrating to the younger boys in the street that he could lift it above his head with only his right index finger. He had even removed the brake cables and brake blocks, having discovered that, if he didn't miscalculate his speed, the metal heel-plates on his boots slowed him down quite well. The bike was so light now it was almost like riding on nothing. Like riding on air. Like flying. Riding the new superlightweight Carlton was the nearest thing to freedom he could find... He arrived at school on the Monday morning in a stream of sparks as he negotiated the turn into the yard and slowed to a graceful stop by the bike shed.

"Hey, Jonesy, feel the weight of that!"

He bawled at a pale youth who was stowing his bike at the back of the shed. Jonesy came out and lifted the Carlton.

"Wow! How d'ya gerrit so light?"

"It's rubbish! It's norra bike - it's a bleeding wreck!"

Pete Crick, a lean and bitter fourth year with lank brown hair that hung over his face, was staring at Young Red from the corner of the shed. He and Young Red had fought three times that year and Young Red had won each time. But Cricksy always pushed his luck.

"It's the lightest bike you've ever seen, Cricksy." Young Red held it up on his finger. "You find one lighter than that!"

Cricksy came up and, a little warily, lifted the bike. "That's nothing," he put the bike down and pushed his hair out of his eyes. "My brother's gorra Raleigh racer what's lighter than yours." He looked disdainfully at Young Red's bike. "Never even heard of a Carlton."

"So what? There's lots of stuff you've never heard." Young Red took a belligerent step towards Cricksy and took his bike back.

"Such as?" Cricksy eyed Young Red enviously from behind his hair.

Young Red stepped up to him and prodded him on the chest. "You've never heard the sound of my fist breaking the bones in your head - but you're never going to forget it!"

"Piss off!" Cricksy took a step backwards, noting a convenient line of flight. "You wanna gerra decent bike afore you come bragging in here! What you laughing at?"

Young Red was looking over his adversary's shoulder. Mouth, who had crept up unnoticed, grabbed Cricksy's arms from behind.

"Here stands Cricksy, who thought he was so tricksy, but along came Red and hit him on his head, and made him feel mighty sicksy! Go on, Red," Mouth laughed. "Plant one on him for me while you're at it!"

Young Red hadn't come to school to fight. He wasn't sure what to do so he didn't do anything. Christ, he thought, you only have to step out of your house and there's trouble, whether you're looking for it or not. He'd only wanted to show off his bike and it had started all this. How could tea leaves and all that witchcraft stuff see the hundreds of things that could happen before nine o'clock in the morning that might change your life for ever? Making sense of anything was impossible. Normally he would have given Cricksy a good thumping, but today, he decided all at once, he would do things differently.

"Leave him."

He pushed his bike into the shed.

"He ain't worth the bother."

Mouth was about to kick Cricksy in the back when his attention was caught by a commotion in the gateway. The yard erupted with shouts and wolf-whistles and every head in the playground turned to look. It was Sally Bell. Mouth, with a mocking grin, pushed Cricksy away and took a step forward, "Here comes Sally Bell - touch her tits and go to hell!"

In her black stockings and high heeled shoes, her short green skirt and tight black sweater Sally Bell was the image of the archetypal seductress. She stopped just inside the gate and surveyed the scene before her as some ancient pagan queen might have contemplated her court. The boys goggled, but the older girls looked askance and frowned.

Mouth's voice came suddenly again, "There stands sexy Sally - for a couple of bob you can bang her in the alley!"

The yard erupted in laughter, which was especially loud among the girls. But Sally Bell's calculated entrance did not crumble. Tossing her heavy blond curls she located the familiar taunting voice by the bike shed. As she crossed the yard in her new high heels the crowd parted like the sea before a divinity.

"Now you know what it's like!" With a sharp crack she slapped Mouth across his face with all the weight of her mature woman's body.

As Mouth fell backwards he grabbed Sally Bell's arm and they both went down together. Before she could free herself Mouth's hand shot under her skirt like some demented tunnelling animal. The bike shed was full of figures, older girls foremost, yelling at Mouth in encouragement:

"Get it in her, Lenny!"

"Screw the bitch till she can't stand up!"

"Hold her down, Red, and we'll all have a go!"

But Young Red hadn't come to hold her down.

"Geroff her, you flaming animal!"

He grabbed Mouth by his belt and jacket collar and, his eyes bulging with effort, dragged him out of the bike shed. Young Red let go of him and stood back, waiting for the knife to spring into his friend's fingers. Mouth knelt up slowly, his expression distracted, his eyes unfocused. But Young Red knew this was Mouth at his most dangerous, when he seemed to be most uncertain. Mouth must have got the message. He grinned up at Young Red and, still kneeling, held his arms out wide, his face a mask of mock contrition.

"Hey, old buddy, let's not fight over a fucking squaw!"

Young Red kept his distance, watching Mouth's hands. He knew, if he turned around, Mouth would be on his back. He could almost feel Mouth's arms tightening around his neck. Mouth had done it before and he'd had to bash him against a wall to get him off.

The nine o'clock bell invaded the yard like an airstrike, scattering the attention of the onlookers. Mouth got to his feet and spat.

"Never meant no harm, Red. Joke just got out of hand, okay? Still friends, right?"

"Right."

Young Red spoke woodenly, keeping his eyes on Mouth's hands. He couldn't trust anyone any more. He could hardly trust himself.

"Tell her I didn't mean nothing."

Mouth's eyes shifted to the bike shed.

"Tell her we'll still get her some cigs."

A hint of a cunning smile twitched at his sallow features.

Young Red nodded. Mouth turned and strode away across the playground. Young Red watched until he disappeared into school, then went to the bike shed and helped the subdued Sally Bell to her feet.

"Thanks, Red." She kept her hand on his arm. "You going in?"

"Dunno. Are you?"

"No. Wanna go for a walk?"

"Why not?"

"We can go to the priory if you like."

He nodded and she squeezed his arm.

To hell with school, he thought. To hell with friends. To hell with everything. Whatever you did it brought trouble. There was nothing you could do to avoid it, whether you tried to do right or wrong. May as well have a bit of fun. It couldn't make things any worse.

Chapter Eleven

The ruined Augustinian priory lay on a raised shelf of land four hundred yards back from the river. It was about a mile from the town and could be reached only on foot, either by a path that followed the river, branching inland at a field gate, or by a narrow overgrown track from the Roman Camp. Young Red couldn't face the sight of the river, so he and Sally Bell took a circuitous route of back lanes and alleys across the town until they arrived at the fence that surrounded the camp.

One of Sally Bell's heels had broken in her fall and she had to sit on Young Red's bike, her tight skirt pulled half way up her thighs, while he held on to the seat and steered her carefully along the lanes and alleys. Sally Bell wasn't used to racing bikes - and certainly not those without brakes - and she shrieked in panic if he forgot and took his hands away. He forgot quite often, distracted by the sight of the bare skin above her stockings and the closeness of her body as he wheeled her through the town. When they reached the fence by the camp Sally Bell dismounted and pulled down her skirt. Young Red felt a sense of loss.

Sally Bell glanced over the fence, "I won't be able to ride on that path, but I can walk barefoot now, Red, it's a nice hot day." She looked up at him anxiously. "You get me any cigs?"

Young Red produced a pack from his jacket pocket. "Keep 'em. I've got some more."

"You must be rich," she smiled at him admiringly.

"I've got a paper round."

"It must be good pay."

She lit a cigarette hurriedly. Young Red noticed that her hands were shaking.

"Good enough."

"Good enough to buy me all these cigs?"

"I do other stuff too," he lied. "Fix bikes for kids and stuff like that."

"Wish I was clever like you," Sally Bell pouted, "I'm not clever at anything."

"But you are, Sal," he protested earnestly. "All that stuff you were saying about what music people like, and how it's changing with young folks having more money to spend and all that. You know loads more than me - you should go on one of them quiz shows and make a lot of money."

Sally Bell shrugged. "Radio Luxembourg's best. I listen to it on a night. Nothing else to do."

"But you remember everything - all the facts - flip sides, backing groups, labels, dates and such." He continued enthusiastically. "And all that stuff you was saying at lunchtimes about different sorts of music, like harmony and instrumentals and ballads. You should get a job in a music shop." He looked puzzled. "Why didn't you bring your radio today?"

"Batteries are done." She giggled. "I got dressed up today instead."

They were silent for a while. Sally Bell stared thoughtfully at the bumpy field.

"You think I'm that good, Red? You know, with music and that?"

"I do, Sal. I thought I knew a fair bit, but you know tons more than me!" Young Red looked at Sally Bell, at her shiny blond curls, her full lips, her perfect body almost bursting from its skintight wrapping. "Anyway, with a figure like that you don't need to be good at anything."

He beamed down at her approvingly.

"Have I got a good figure, Red?" She glanced up at him, her mouth slightly open, uncertain if he would say what she wanted to hear.

"Best figure this side of Marilyn Monroe!"

They blushed at each other. Sally Bell giggled and shook her curls, leaning back against the fence. Young Red accepted the invitation and they kissed a little awkwardly. Sally Bell's hair smelled of smoke. After a while he straightened up while she lit another cigarette.

"You don't half get through some cigs, Sal. You'll get like Connie Potter. My mam was saying she coughs that bad in a morning she drops down in a faint."

Young Red looked at his companion with concern. Sally Bell stared towards the sunlit river, which wound like a silver ribbon through the distant fields.

"I can't help it, Red. I get all trembly and I have to have a cig. I've been like that since my dad got killed in the wool press and they took my mam to the mental hospital when she had her breakdown afterwards. If I don't have a cig I just start crying and... and I can't stop." She looked up at him and her face coloured. "Don't tell anyone, though, Red, will you? It's just between you and me."

Young Red shook his head, touched that she should confide in him something so personal. He understood her need for those soothing bandages of smoke.

"Promise?"

She squeezed his hand, suddenly anxious in case he mocked her. "Don't tell Len or anyone."

Young Red smiled gently down at her, moved by her trust. He could never speak of his own dark past to a living soul.

"Promise."

"Anyway..." she laughed and tossed her curls, "Connie Potter's old. She must be thirty-five!"

They kissed again. Young Red hadn't been alone with Sally Bell in such unconfined circumstances before. There was so much more to her, he realised, than the dirty girl from lunchtimes in the Swamp. He pulled away from her and looked around, "Better get going or someone'll spot us."

They crossed the Roman Camp and walked in single file on the bumpy path through the fields, Sally Bell carrying her shoes and Young Red with the crossbar of the Carlton resting on his shoulder.

"Good job it's a light bike, or I'd have to leave it in a ditch."

"You can carry it, Red. You're strong! You pulled Len off me as if he was a doll!"

Sally Bell turned and said seriously, "I'll never forget that, Red. People don't do stuff like that for me."

Young Red flexed his left bicep, "I'm the Coffee Bar Kid, remember!"

116

He didn't laugh because she didn't. They looked at each other with quiet solemnity.

Sally Bell was in front. Young Red watched her natural swaying rhythm as she walked confidently, barefoot, on the beaten earth of the path. The buildings of the town receded and the drone of machines began to fade. Sand martins skimmed over the pastures between the footpath and the river, hunting for insects. As he watched the stupendous aerobatics of the birds Young Red remembered Mouth's condemnation of nature on the day of the flood. He looked from the birds to his companion, but he didn't feel the slightest lessening of his sense of awe. Walking through the fields with a lovely girl was as amazing as birdflight. Mouth was wrong. Nature wasn't just a breeding machine. Nature was beautiful. Like Sally Bell.

As they approached the priory Young Red could see the houses of the council estate where Sally Bell lived with her aunt and where the ted with the flick-knife nursed his wounded pride. The estate was not yet finished; he could see in the distance figures on scaffolding moving around new houses without roofs. It'll be down to the priory one day like folks say, he thought. Then we won't have the place to ourselves any more.

He lifted his bike over the ramshackle fence that surrounded the ruins then helped Sally Bell in her inappropriate skirt.

"Why d'you come to school all dolled up like that? If Mouth hadn't said something the teachers would have."

"Oh..." she looked confused and blushed. "It were just an idea I had. But it didn't work. I just felt like dressing up. It don't matter anyway - we'll be finished with school by the end of next week."

She paused, then added, almost as an afterthought, "They're not my things. They're Josie's."

"What d'you want to wear your aunt's things for?"

Sally Bell pouted, "Oh, I just felt like it. Josie don't wear them any more... She didn't want me to either, but..." she ended defiantly, "but I wore them anyway." She smiled provocatively at Young Red. "I look better in 'em than she did, 'cos she's so thin."

117

Young Red stopped asking questions. He knew from experience with his sister that women became annoyed if you asked them too much. They don't like questions, he thought, because they're women and they don't want to know why they do things. He had to carry Sally Bell from the fence to the cloister, because the spiky grass prickled her feet. He didn't notice her weight, he was so overcome by her closeness; he could feel her breasts moving against his chest and her clear blue eyes were only inches from his own. He prattled uncharacteristically in his embarrassment.

"You don't know how lucky you are being a woman. If a bloke had hit Mouth like you did he'd have ended up in hospital. Not right then, maybe. But later. He's dangerous, Mouth is. He remembers stuff like that. There's only two people safe in his company and that's himself and his dad. And I'm not too sure about the first one, neither."

He didn't mention Mouth's apology. He wanted her to hate him. He didn't want Mouth near her ever again.

He left Sally Bell on the softer grass in the cloister and hurried back for his bike, which he hid in a little side chapel off the north transept. When he got back to the cloister Sally Bell was in her bra and panties, blushing.

Young Red could hardly approach her. Up to now he had only touched her with her clothes on. Even last September, when he and Mouth had come to the priory with her one Saturday afternoon they had got no further than touching her breasts, whatever Mouth had said to all and sundry afterwards. She had never taken her clothes off in front of them. Young Red was still in his blue windcheater. He took it off and held it out to her, "Here - sit on this."

"I'll have to have a cig, Red," Sally Bell blushed even more. "I'm all shaky. I've never done it with anyone afore."

She lit a cigarette and sat on the windcheater, drawing her knees up to her chest. Young Red knelt beside her.

"You want to do it?" His voice had never spoken those words before. His brain stopped working then and he was only aware of the state of his body, which felt stretched tight as a drumskin.

His head felt numb, as if it had been set in stone. It was as if there was a second, bigger Young Red inside him who had kept out of sight all his life, but who now had risen to the surface, threatening to burst through his flesh like someone outgrowing a garment.

"Come on, Red, take off your things," Sally Bell suggested with a hint of impatience. Blindly he obeyed, until he stood before her self-consciously in his underpants. Sally Bell finished her cigarette and took off her bra.

"Come on, Red. You take your pants off and I'll take mine off - both together."

He took off his underpants and knelt beside her. He was devastated before her unclothed body. He didn't want to move, just sit in the grass and stare for ever at her incredible nakedness. She put out her tongue and uttered a little snort of pleasure when she realised the depth of his fascination. Then she moved her hand and she must have touched him, because a ripple of energy shot through his body. He didn't dare to look at what she was doing. The next time she did it, it was too much. He grabbed her and she clutched him and they pressed their bodies together and smothered their faces in each other's hair. After a while they looked at each other and made a few cautious explorations. When they were sure where their respective body-parts were they embraced again. After several brief wrestlings they managed to fit themselves together perfectly. Sally Bell screamed and Young Red groaned and exploded.

They rolled apart and kissed and embraced and examined each other's bodies as minutely as if they were the only human beings on earth and had only just found each other after wandering alone for years on an empty planet. They looked at the blood on Young Red's penis and Sally Bell's legs. Young Red was horrified.

"Oh, Christ, Sal, have I hurt you?"

"Just a bit - but that's normal. Hasn't anyone ever told you what happens to a woman when she loses her virginity?"

Young Red dabbed at the blood with his handkerchief, while Sally Bell explained what had happened. He watched her face as she talked. He wanted to kiss her a thousand times, but was afraid to in case she thought he was a sissy. After a while they wanted to do it again and slid together more easily this time. When they came Young Red kissed her and Sally Bell whispered his name in his ear, over and over, like a secret initiatory spell.

The sun was so warm they dozed off briefly, rolled tightly together. When they woke up they looked at each other in silence, then stood up and put on their clothes.

"I'm so thirsty, Red. Where's that spring we found last year?"

"Dunno. Think it's outside the walls by a tree."

They found the spring on a low bank under a hawthorn and took it in turns to drink, gasping at the coldness of the water. Then they sat on a ruined wall in the sun. Sally Bell took Young Red's hand and squeezed it gently. "I'm not like what Len says I am. You believe that, Red?"

He looked at her anxious face and nodded.

"I haven't any friends 'cos the girls all think I get off with lots of lads. You know - with Ingo and them. But I ain't been with no-one 'cept you. You know that now, don't you?"

He nodded, watching her face.

"It's all 'cos of what Len said." She lit a cigarette and looked up at him earnestly. "Len hates me, don't he, Red? Is it 'cos of his mam? I mean, going off with another bloke? She looked like me a bit, didn't she?

"Dunno. Could be." Young Red fingered the scar on his cheek, a habit he had developed when he was trying to get things clear in his head. "He's funny, is Mouth. Don't know where you are with him most of the time."

"D'you think he'll hurt me for what I did to him this morning?"

"He won't dare, 'cos he knows I'll sort him out. Anyway, he ain't that bad." He smiled at her reassuringly; Sally Bell still looked worried.

"Can I ask you something, Red?"

"Sure."

She pulled his head gently towards her and pressed her lips to his scar.

120

"Red, will you look after me... one day... if no-one else'll have me - when I get old like Connie Potter?"

"Course, Sal. Just give me a shout." He smiled and squeezed her hand.

They wandered around among the ruins, stopping to kiss and embrace several times, until they arrived at a circular arrangement of stones set in the ground almost completely obscured by a pile of old sun-bleached planks. Young Red stopped and stared, lost in his thoughts.

"What's that, Red? Was someone going to have a bonfire?"

Young Red lifted the end of a plank with the toe of his boot and peered down.

"It's the old well. Shack says it's a hundred foot deep. His dad covered it with these boards in case anyone fell in."

Sally Bell took a step backwards from the circle of stones.

"What did they want a well for when they had a spring?"

"Dunno. Mebbe the spring went dry odd times."

Young Red lifted the end of another plank.

"Shack said once when he was a lad his dad winched him down and he found a skelinton at the bottom. It were a bloke who did himself in twenty year afore. Shack said they found out from his teeth."

Sally Bell shuddered.

"C'mon, Red. It's horrible. Let's go and lie in the sun."

She started walking back towards the cloister. Young Red stood musing, staring at the planks on top of the well, then he ambled after her, catching her up at the top of the chapter house steps. He encircled her waist with his arm.

"You know, Sal... that time when Mouth and me and Brock was having that row in the Swamp - that time when Mouth hit you for snooping..."

"I weren't snooping!" She pulled away from him, pouting angrily. He faced her in the cloister doorway.

"No - that's just what Mouth said. I know you weren't snooping... That time, anyway... when we had that row with Brock... well... what d'you think we was doing?"

"Having a row."

"Yes... but what d'you think we was saying?" He tried to sound as casual as he could, so his voice wouldn't betray his sense of urgency.

"Oh... nothing." She frowned and looked away over the ruins towards the river. "I never heard nothing... Only Brock saying he weren't there and it had nothing to do with him. Something like that." She added petulantly, "I only came for a cig."

Young Red breathed a sigh of relief. "Okay. That's okay. It don't matter now anyway."

"What were you planning to do - rob a bank, or something?" Sally Bell laughed up at him.

"Jesus - no!" Young Red laughed too, a little awkwardly. "It were only a row about... about nothing really." He turned into the cloister. "Shit! I left my jacket behind! It's a good job there's no-one about."

"There's never anyone about." Sally Bell followed him into the cloister. "I come down here sometimes to get away from Josie. She's always nagging about how much I smoke and stuff." She sat on Young Red's jacket.

"You come down here on your own?" Young Red was amazed. "What if someone grabs you?"

"I don't care. No-one cares..." She ran her fingers through her jumbled hair. "I just have to get away... You don't know what it's like to have someone nagging at you every minute you're inside. Always on about how to live and what I should be doing and thinking and everything."

Young Red felt a deep sympathy for Sally Bell. But he didn't say a word.

"I come down here on a little path from the end of the estate. I hate that estate! It were better when I lived in town with my dad and mam... Anyway, there's only Shack down here - and his dad, of course - and they're that old fashioned they'd think it were wrong even to think about touching me. Shack's dad let me have a go on his pipe once though," she laughed at the recollection, "but it made me cough."

"Probably a mixture of chicken shit and tree bark!"

"He said it were rosemary and something else... I've forgot... But I didn't like it."

After a while they undressed again and made love in the sunny cloister. When they woke from a prolonged doze Young Red searched his jacket pockets for his watch.

"It's a good job it's got a strong face, we might have broke it with all that rolling about."

He found it and stared at it. "It's okay... Jesus - it's nearly six o'clock!"

Sally Bell yawned and stretched. "You can't tell if it's getting late in summer, 'cos it stays so hot."

Young Red was struggling into his clothes. "My dad'll have a fit. I'll be late for tea. It'll take me half an hour to get home carrying my bike."

Sally Bell located her aunt's high heeled shoes.

"Josie'll kill me for breaking her heel. You any money, Red - so I can get it mended? Josie don't even need to know."

Young Red looked at the shoe. "Only wants gluing. I'll do it tomorrer in woodwork."

He stuffed the shoe into his jacket pocket.

"Thanks, Red. You're always saving me."

She pulled him towards her and they kissed.

"We can do it again on Saturday, if you like."

Young Red nodded. "Why not? Ten o'clock?"

"Okay. But get some rubber whatsits, Red. It was all right today 'cos I'd just finished my period. But get some whatsits for next time."

"I'll get them from the barber's."

"And some cigs, Red. Don't forget."

He helped her over the fence and she set off across the fields towards the estate. Young Red watched her meandering through the grass, carrying her aunt's shoe. Pity it had to end, he thought. We could have gone on like that for ever. But, still, there was Saturday...

Tea was almost finished by the time Young Red got home. As soon as he walked in Janet fled upstairs to her room to get out of

123

the way. Young Red felt angry, buoyed up by his day with Sally Bell. You try to please yourself for once, he thought, and you have to face some kind of criminal trial... He hung his jacket on the back of the kitchen door, next to Big Red's boiler suit, which gleamed dully with grease like ancient armour. He bit his lip and stepped into the dining room.

"Now then, lad," his father put his cup down loudly in its saucer. His white shirt looked crisp and newly ironed; it was unbuttoned at the neck, Big Red never wore a tie. "What sort of time d'you call this?"

"I've been worried sick about you, Ronnie," his mother stood up from the table. "With that lad of Bottomleys disappearing, and not a hair of him seen since, I didn't know what to think! Then there was that business in the coffee bar... Times are getting more violent. Anything can happen to a lad out on his own."

Young Red's stomach tied itself in a knot at the mention of Raggy.

"Had a puncture. Had to go to Chris Marsden's to fix it." He stared sullenly at the flower patterned tablecloth. "Anyway, I can look after myself."

"Punctures be buggered!" The pitch of Big Red's voice set off a resonant echo from something in the kitchen. "Why didn't you mend it here?"

"Run out of patches - have to get some more tomorrer." Young Red turned to his mother. "Sorry I'm late. Is there anything left for me?"

He was hungrier than he had been for weeks.

"There's some soup and a couple of dumplings - but I think your father wants to speak to you afore you have your tea." Nancy fixed him with a worried frown.

"Speak! You're bloody right I want to speak!" Big Red bellowed. "You know what day it is, lad?"

"Monday thirteenth of July."

His father gave Young Red a withering stare. "What else?"

"It's a schoolday."

For a sickening moment Young Red thought they might have been looking for him and Sally Bell.

"Course it's a bloody schoolday! You've got nine of them left. Then, in September, you go to work. Right? Haven't forgot about Reeds, have you?" Big Red's sarcasm was scathing. He released a burst of short sentences like a spray of machine-gun fire, "Union meeting. Tonight. I arranged it last week. Right? So's you can learn the ropes."

"Oh, sh... " Young Red put his hand to the scar on his face. His heart dropped like a stone down an ancient well. "Sorry, Dad - I forgot. Can't go anyway. Have to fix this kid's bike." The lie was out before he had time to think. He went on quickly, "Need the money. Saving up." He stared at the tablecloth.

"Bikes be blasted!" Big Red's heavy gaze settled on the top of his son's bowed head. Young Red could feel it there like a steady pressure. "The union's the future! That's your saving up! That's your insurance! You've got to learn the ropes, lad - learn whose side you're on! When you step into that furnace house in September you'll think you've walked into hell. It ain't the bosses'll save you - it's union solidarity! We're the only salvation - the only dignity - the working man has got!"

Young Red weathered the onslaught. He was in hell already - a hell more tortured than Reeds. He thought of Sally Bell, of her pain and loneliness, which was so much closer to him now and it gave him courage. He thought of their lovemaking and it fuelled his defiance. He thought of the inescapable sadness that was everywhere, that he had first noticed when he left the police station and it generated a kind of reckless despair.

"Sorry, Dad. Can't turn work away. Thinking of making it into a bit of a sideline."

"You're a capitalist in nappies!" Big Red roared. Young Red could feel his mother wilting in her chair as his father's wrath continued. "You'll be chasing money for ever! A full time job and a couple of sidelines and you still won't have enough! Union's the only way to get a fair deal! Only way to make sense of your life!" He paused, glaring at Young Red. "If you let me down again, lad, you can whistle for your job at Reeds! You might make yourself into a fool - but you won't make me into one too! I have a position there. I have respect. I won't have a son of mine acting like an idiot under my nose! You keep on behaving the way you are and you can get out! Go and live with Old Florrie - you're about as daft as her..."

"Red!" His mother was angry too. "I won't hear you say those things about my mother!" Nancy stood up again and almost threw down her teaspoon. "See what you've done to this house!" She waved her finger at Young Red. "See what you're doing to us with your ridiculous ways!"

Young Red glared at them both. But his mother's rebuke cut him deeper than his father's rage. How could she take Big Red's side against him? How could she? Without a word he grabbed his jacket and was half way down the street on the Carlton before his mother's voice reached him from the backyard gate. But he didn't turn around. He cycled fast as far as the Roman Camp and flung himself down in the bumpy field and pounded the earth with his fists.

"Bastard!" he yelled at the earth. "Bitch!"

Another row like that, he thought, and I'll go and get Sally Bell and we'll go away together to... He couldn't think where they would go. But wherever they went, he knew, it would be better than here. He would cut his connections, like Old Florrie had said. With a shock he realised exactly what she had meant. Yes, he thought, I'll go. I'll get clear of this rotten life - and I'll get my life clear.

After a while he calmed down. He sat on the grass in the evening sun thinking of the girl he had been with all day. Eventually he went home. His father and sister were out and his mother was ironing. He could see she had been crying. He ate a slice of bread and cheese in the kitchen and thought of Mouth, making his bread and cheese sandwiches every day in his dismal house. This is what it's like for him, he thought, the same thing every time you eat. Suppose life is what you get used to... When he had finished eating he walked stiffly past his mother and went to bed, hoping he would dream all night of Sally Bell.

Before he got into bed he switched off the light. He didn't need lights on any more. Raggy could go to hell - he wasn't afraid. He preferred to dream of Sally Bell in the dark.

Chapter Twelve

Saturday the eighteenth of July dawned bright and sunny. Just right, Young Red thought as he dressed. Just perfect. In a stream of sparks from his studded heels he slowed the Carlton to make the turn into the alley at the side of Ralph Parnaby's shop. He stopped by the back door and tried the handle. Good. Ralph had already unlocked the door and, he hoped, gone back to bed as usual. Lazy old bugger, Young Red thought, serves him right if we run things our way. He opened the door and went in, standing for a moment in the silence. Good. The shop was empty; Ralph had gone back to sleep.

Young Red wanted to put his plan into action before Mouth arrived at the shop. Carefully he took two packs of cigarettes from the stacks on the shelves behind the counter, one pack from each of two separate stacks. Forty. That should be enough. He was doing Mouth's part of the operation this morning - strictly against union regulations. But to hell with unions. The only way you ever got anywhere was to change the rules to suit yourself.

As he was dragging the bundles of papers inside from the street he heard a squeal of brakes in the alley and a moment later Mouth's scowling figure appeared in the shop.

"Done anything?" Mouth's eyes were bloodshot from lack of sleep. Must have been helping his dad at a dog-fight till the early hours. He'll be in a bad mood, Young Red thought. Better be careful.

"Course not. Anyway I'm not seeing Belly today. Going for a bike ride soon as I've done my round."

"Like hell you are!" Mouth vaulted the counter, ignoring the bolted half door at the end and began helping himself to packs of cigarettes. He took one pack from the tops of three different stacks.

"Quick - put these in your jacket afore Dilly and Dally get here and piss in their pants!"

Young Red didn't move. He looked at Mouth in dismay. "Shit, Mouth, we don't need sixty! They'll be missed!" He took a step backwards away from the counter. "Anyway, I told you, I'm going for a bike ride."

"Put the fucking things in your jacket!" Mouth snarled. "We're off to the priory today with Belly."

Young Red was dumbfounded. "Since when?"

Mouth's rubber mask twitched with vexation. "Saw her last night. After school." He added stonily, "It's arranged, okay?"

Young Red's spirits sank out of sight. So much for his perfect day. Sally Bell must have told Mouth of their plans - but how? Why? She hated him, didn't she? Well, didn't she?

He resisted the temptation to spit in Mouth's face, or to kick hell out of the bundles of papers.

"Just give me a couple of packs. I'm not taking sixty."

"They're our insurance!" Mouth glowered, holding out the packs of cigarettes.

"Stuff you! You sound like my dad!"

"Bollocks! Take them!"

"No. Forty."

"Sixty. Be quick!"

"Shit!"

Young Red, unnerved and guilt-ridden, snatched the cigarettes and put them in his pockets. He tried another move.

"Belly don't know anything - you know - about that time with Brock. We don't have to do this."

He started cutting the strings on the bundles of papers with his clasp-knife, passing them to Mouth who arranged them on the counter.

Mouth frowned. "How you find out?"

"I asked her. After we had that... that fight. We went for a walk and I asked her."

"Like hell you did!" Mouth's face was a mass of conflicting emotions - so many Young Red didn't know what to make of it. "Mebbe you went for a walk - but then you screwed her!"

Young Red was bewildered and furious. "Who said?"

"She did. Last night. Said you screwed her seven times!" Mouth's face contorted into a mask of contempt curiously mingled with violent lust.

128

"Shit!" Young Red put his fingers to the scar on his left cheek. He felt betrayed and outraged. "I don't believe you!" he yelled in desperation.

"Ask her!"

"I will!"

Mouth sneered, "Same as you asked her about Brock?"

"What d'you mean?"

"I mean you can't trust a woman. They'll say anything what suits them." Mouth's face became momentarily still as he looked Young Red straight in the eye. "No-one'll ever know what Belly heard till she makes up her mind to tell. You'd better hope, when it comes out, it makes no more sense than the rest of the rubbish in her head!"

A thunderous tattoo on the floor above their heads cut their conversation short.

"Shit! We've woke Ralph up. Let's get going."

With practised speed they sorted the papers into the order of their rounds and hoisted the heavy paper-bags on to their shoulders. They wheeled their bikes out of the alley and stood in the deserted market square.

"What was it like, then?" Mouth leered at Young Red. "Was she a good screw?"

Young Red's former possessive mood had completely gone. He felt depressed. He could think of no reason to protect Sally Bell any more.

"She was all right. We only had it three times and she was a virgin."

Mouth exploded with incredulity. "Lying sod! She's no more a virgin than my dad's bull terrier bitch!"

"I tell you." Young Red stated flatly. "She was a virgin."

Mouth looked at him in amazement. Young Red was amused to see such an unfamiliar emotion on his friend's face.

"She can't have been." Mouth's lips curled in a sneer. "She's been with all sorts."

"Such as? Name at least two."

Young Red was enjoying his friend's confusion. Mouth had swallowed his own tales about Sally Bell completely.

"Ingo for a start."

Young Red shook his head, smiling omnisciently.

"Chick-Chick and Thomo, then."

Young Red shook his head again.

"She's been with... with us!"

Mouth was growing desperate and Young Red laughed.

"Bollocks! We only felt her up a bit with her undies on!"

Mouth was at a loss and Young Red was triumphant.

"And I'll tell you something else. She has a little white mark, same size as the end of my fingernail, just above her place - and the hair's different there, too. A sort of pale goldy colour and stiffer."

Mouth was silent for a minute. He cleared his throat and spat into the gutter.

"Well, Red," he spoke at last with supreme disdain. "Looks like you must have done it."

"Course." Young Red shrugged. "It was no big deal."

Mouth was suddenly businesslike.

"Look after them cigs, Red." He grinned maliciously. "We need to be sure we keep her under our thumb." He swung his leg over his old black Raleigh. "See you at the Roman Camp at half nine, okay? And don't bring your bloody bike!"

He creaked slowly away across the market square to begin his round.

She must have told him about the bike, too, Young Red thought. Mouth was right - she couldn't be trusted. You couldn't trust anyone with anything ever.

Mouth and Young Red strolled through the pastures between the Roman Camp and the priory. The sun was already very warm and Young Red took off his windcheater and swung it over his shoulder.

"Might get a bit of a sun tan today," he mused, glancing into the sky.

"You've changed your jacket." Mouth looked at him in alarm.

"It's okay. I've got the cigs. All sixty."

"Who's going first?"

"Dunno," Young Red shrugged.

He felt indifferent. He was here to protect his own future, he had decided, that was all; to make sure Belly stayed mum. "You, if you want."

Mouth spat, "No - you go first, Red. Warm her up a bit." His grin failed to displace the furrows of doubt above his eyes. Young Red observed them and took note.

"Fair enough. Me first." He added sternly, "And no watching!"

Sally Bell was sitting in a niche in the cloister wall when they arrived. She smiled a little sheepishly at Young Red. She was wearing a flower patterned summer dress.

"Give us a cig, Red, I'm all of a tremble. Did you get any whatsits?"

Young Red nodded and gave her a pack of Senior Service. He turned to Mouth, who was kicking the grass-heads with his heavy black boots - he never wore shoes, even at weekends.

"Give you a shout in a bit."

Mouth grinned wickedly and sauntered out of the cloister, kicking the grass-heads as he went. He had hardly even glanced at Sally Bell.

"What the hell you telling him stuff for?" Young Red turned angrily on her when Mouth had gone.

"Sorry, Red." She avoided his eyes. "I lost my temper with him and it just came out. He were saying all sorts of lying things about me after school yesterday." She pouted. "You should have been there to look after me."

"I can't be everywhere!" he exploded. "I had to take some stuff up to my gran's!"

"Don't be angry at me, Red. I didn't mean to tell." A large tear slid down her face. "It were just that he were so horrible to me and he needed putting in his place."

A second tear followed the first. At the sight of her tears Young Red was too moved to speak.

"He's only a kid and I told him! He's never done anything with a woman. He ain't a man like you."

She drew him to her and they embraced. But the thought of Mouth skulking among the ruins made Young Red pull away.

"He'll want it too, you know. He ain't come down here for his summer holidays."

Sally Bell seemed resigned. "We'll just do it once - quick - and then you come back. I won't let him do it again."

"You promise?"

Young Red asked doubtfully. She smiled at him and stuck out her tongue.

"Promise."

The sight of Sally Bell's flower patterned dress was getting on Young Red's nerves.

"Take that thing off." He tugged at the zip on the back of the dress. "What d'you want to wear a thing like that for?"

He sounded more stern than he had intended. Sally Bell looked hurt.

"Josie got it for me from a sale. I thought I looked good in it."

"It reminds me of tea time."

They made love in the warm grass. Afterwards Young Red felt dejected, not buoyant like the first time. He wondered if it would ever be as good again as on that unexpected sunny Monday. Funny how things change. Today was supposed to have been so different from the way it was turning out. He couldn't do it again without a rest, so he decided to find Mouth. Anyway he knew if he didn't they would risk an unpleasant interruption.

He stood up.

"I'll get him."

He pulled on his pants. Sally Bell looked worried.

"Don't go too far off, Red. He might get rough."

"Just give me a shout."

Young Red found Mouth at the old well, on his hands and knees peering under a plank into the darkness. He had known he would be there.

"Making sure it's deep enough for all the folk you're going to have to kill when Belly blabs." He gave Young Red a twisted grin.

"Piss off!" Young Red glanced towards the cloister. "Anyway, she's waiting."

Mouth stood up. "My turn, then. Give us the cigs."

Young Red handed him a pack of Kensitas.

"Can I do what I like?"

"Long as she wants to."

Mouth hesitated. "I've got an idea."

He beckoned Young Red and they wandered together back to the cloister. Sally Bell, dressed again, stood up in surprise when she saw them both in the cloister doorway.

"What's up? Someone about?"

"Going to play a game." Mouth grinned crookedly at Sally Bell. Young Red, standing behind him, caught her eye and shrugged.

"We'll give you two minutes by Red's time-bomb and when it explodes we're coming to find you. First one to find her has her for an hour. Okay?"

Sally Bell stared at them. "You wanna do this, Red?"

Young Red shrugged.

"But where can I hide?"

"Anywhere you can get to in two minutes." Mouth tried to smile at her, but the attempt turned into a grimace.

"Okay." Sally Bell giggled. The idea seemed to appeal to her. "When do I start?"

Young Red held the old Ingersoll so that Mouth could see it. Mouth counted, "Ten, nine, eight..."

Young Red frowned.

"Seven, six, five..."

Sally Bell giggled.

"Four, three, two, one - go!"

Sally Bell shrieked as she ran through the cloister grass. Mouth chanted, "Sally Bell, you'd better be quick, old Red's coming for you with his great big..."

"Pack it in!" Young Red rounded on him angrily. "You start that business and I'm off! It's a stupid game anyway."

"Too late," Mouth mocked him. "She's gone. Anyway, you'll find her first, Red, 'cos she'll show herself to you."

There was no resentment in Mouth's face, only contempt. Young Red was puzzled by his friend's attitude. He looked at his watch.

"One minute." He began to be assailed with doubts. "Look, Mouth, it's a bad idea. Let's call it off."

Mouth raised his dark eyebrows in surprise. "What's wrong with a bit of sport? Thought you liked a spot of hunting, Red?"

"If you find her, you'd better not hurt her."

"Scout's honour." Mouth saluted him and laughed.

"Time's up."

"Sally Bell!" Mouth yelled. "We're coming to find you! You'd better watch out, 'cos I'm right behind you!"

They set off in opposite directions from the cloister doorway. Young Red lost sight of Mouth almost immediately. He tried to think logically: where would Sally Bell go? Then the thought struck him that women weren't logical people, so she could have gone anywhere. He tried to imagine what it would be like in her position: which way would she have run? But he couldn't imagine anyone so beautiful and strange and sad as Sally Bell. She probably knew the place as well as he did, because she had come here on her own... But would she have explored; would she have looked in all the nooks and crannies? Young Red was at a loss to know where to look. Shit! It was a stupid game. He should have refused to play.

It was a big site. He hadn't realised the extent of the ruins before - there were a thousand places a person could hide... Young Red searched behind pillars. He looked into alcoves, recesses and niches. He peered around doorways, stared into the darkness at the tops of broken stairs.

A few times he thought he had found her, but it was only the movement of grasses in the wind, or a bird dislodging stone dust as it took off in fright from the top of a wall. After a while he stood still and listened. It was so quiet... There was only the sighing of the wind and the distant calling of a gull. It was as if Mouth and Sally Bell had never existed.

She wouldn't go near the well. That was certain. Therefore the chapter house and the rooms beyond it were probably also out of the question as places she would choose to hide - in fact, whatever lay in that direction. But he had looked everywhere else... Young Red found himself back in the cloister again, almost in despair. He glanced at his watch: she had been gone almost fifteen minutes. But where?

He wandered through the north aisle and sat on the base of a ruined pillar. He drummed his heels against the ancient stone and listened to the wind and the insistent calling of the gull. It must be rough weather on the coast for a gull to come this far inland... The sound of the wind and the bird evoked the feeling he had known before of being alone on an alien planet. But the presence of the stones reassured him - though they belonged to a time as distant and irretrievable as a dream.

Perhaps he should shout to the others and call the game off. But there was no point in giving up because, as far as he knew, Mouth might not have fared any better. He was surprised he hadn't seen any sign of him either - not even the most fleeting glimpse - since they had separated at the start of the hunt. He began looking again in places he had searched already: the transepts; the little chapel where he had put his bike - all those years ago last Monday... The chapel had seemed a likely spot for Sally Bell to hide - he had felt certain she would be there when he first looked in. He peered again through the half-light of the little room - and there, among the rubble on the floor, was something he recognised. He picked it up. It was the packet of Capstan, empty now, that he had given her yesterday at school.

She had been here but then she had moved. Why? Which way? Out through that broken wall, perhaps, and over the grass to that separate part of the ruins, with its tumbled stonework in a darker more sombre colour... Young Red set off across the grass towards the monks' old guest house. It was the only spot he hadn't thought to look, because it hardly offered anything in the way of good places to hide. He could hear the gull again, screaming; he looked up but couldn't see it. What was wrong with the stupid bird? Then he set off running flat out across the grass, because the note of the gull's call had changed and become undeniably human...

He found them in the guest house in a corner of an inner room. Mouth sprang away from Sally Bell as Young Red burst in on them.

"What the hell you done to her, you animal? You fucking..." Young Red lost touch with words. The sight of Sally Bell cowering in the corner, her face rigid with terror, stunned him as if he had run headlong into a wall.

"It's okay, Red. She's all right. It were only another game." Mouth protested, backing into the doorway. Young Red ignored him. He crouched beside Sally Bell and made to lift her, or stroke her hair, or soothe her, he couldn't remember which later. But she shrank away from him, wedging herself as tightly as she could into the angle of the corner. She made a small whimpering sound and stared at him with blank terrified eyes.

"What d'you say, Sal?" Young Red bent closer. "I didn't hear you." He spoke gently and smiled, though he felt afraid himself, he had never seen anyone look so strange.

Sally Bell started to shake, first her hands, then her teeth began to chatter. Young Red heard Mouth close behind him and he turned around in fury. "Keep away, you fucking animal! Keep away or I'll kill you!"

Without a word Mouth vanished from the ruined room.

Little by little Young Red coaxed back Sally Bell's attention. He offered her a cigarette and, after a while, she took it from him and smoked in silence, staring at nothing. When she had finished the cigarette she stood up unaided, though she was groggy and leaned on the wall.

"No - don't touch me." Her voice was hoarse and husky, barely audible. It was from her shrieking, Young Red realised afterwards.

"I'm off home now." She brushed vaguely at the dust and grit on her dress. "I never want to see neither of you again."

"But, Sal..."

"Don't touch me!" She hissed at him like a cornered cat. "Nobody touch me!"

Young Red stood back and let her pass. He followed her out of the ruined guest house, keeping a few paces behind. Mouth was nowhere to be seen.

"But, Sal, it had nothing to do with me." He addressed the back of the flower patterned dress. She turned around. Her eyes met his briefly then glanced away.

"Yes it did! You're both a couple of criminals!"

She spat the words at him.

"Leaving me with him when I were screaming and screaming!"

"But, Sal, I didn't... I mean I thought..."

"You're both as bad! Starting that fight in the coffee bar! And shooting that poor Ricky Bottomley!"

Young Red was rocked on his feet. "How'd you know that?"

"I heard all about it. That day. I were snooping - remember?"

"Oh, shit!" Young Red's mind seemed to be spinning like a whirligig.

"And when Josie finds out what he tried to do to me they'll lock the pair of you up!" She turned her back on him and walked away.

"But, Sal - you can't tell her!" Young Red ran after Sally Bell in consternation.

"Don't touch me!" She faced him squarely now. "I'm going to tell Josie he tried to kill me and that you're both mad and you killed Ricky Bottomley and left him in the river and ought to be put away for ever!"

Young Red felt sick. He leaned on a ruined wall and watched Sally Bell walk away. He watched her climb the priory fence and disappear across the fields towards the council estate. After a while he noticed Mouth watching him from the top of a shattered column. That bastard, he thought, he's destroyed me. But he was in it too.

They sat together on the cracked remains of the chancel steps. Young Red couldn't bear the sight of the cloister.

"It were only a game, Red. She just took it the wrong way. I only meant to frighten her a bit." Mouth looked so woebegone Young Red almost believed him. "You should have gone after her and brung her back."

"Too late now. She'll be at home." Young Red looked at his watch. "Nearly half past twelve. Anyway, how could I stop her? I daren't put a finger on her!"

"Okay. Okay." Mouth's forehead creased into furrows of concentration. After a while he cleared his throat and spat. "She won't tell her aunt. You know why?" he grinned cunningly at Young Red, who stared at him blank as a shutter. Since his scene with Sally Bell he hadn't been able to think at all.

"She won't tell 'cos her aunt'll want to know what she were doing down here with us. And she won't tell about that day with Brock 'cos her aunt'll want to know what she were doing snooping in the Swamp. And it won't be long till she runs out of cigs and she won't have no money to get them. So she'll come whining to us."

Young Red would have felt sorry for Sally Bell's plight, but he had too many problems of his own.

"I hope you're right."

"If I'm right or wrong they can't try you for a killing without a body."

Young Red looked doubtful. "If she tells her aunt they might start dragging the river again."

"Nah."

Mouth's face was full of contempt.

"She won't tell. She needs us more than we need her. We got the cigs. We got our insurance. Anyway," he eyed Young Red with a mixture of pity and disdain, "she's yours now. I don't want anything to do with the lying bitch!"

After a long silence Young Red found his tongue, "Didn't you make it, then?"

"Course I did!" Mouth leered savagely. "I screwed the bitch till she lost her bloody voice!"

But there was something in Mouth's manner at odds with his words: something hollow, something dark and desperate. Young Red didn't believe him. He came to torment her, he thought. That's all he enjoys. Because Sally Bell reminds him of his mam.

"Give us one of them posh cigs, Red, it'll help me walk back better."

Young Red handed Mouth his pack of Du Maurier.

"Still pals, right?"

"Right." Young Red replied absently. He couldn't care less at that moment if Mouth was his friend or not. He felt tired and helpless and his head was still reeling.

"Even after all what's happened with Belly?" Mouth's frown-lines creased into abject apology.

"S'pose so."

"We're in it together, aren't we - me and you?" Mouth persisted.

"Course."

But Young Red knew, in spite of all Mouth had to say, he could never trust either of them again. Sally Bell would sell him short when it suited her and Mouth would destroy them both and say it had just been a game.

CHAPTER THIRTEEN

On Saturday evening Young Red went to the pictures. Chris Marsden wasn't in so he went alone. He had to do something. The business at the priory was having a delayed action effect and he felt more and more unsettled as the hours passed. He walked straight into the cinema without bothering to find out what was on and forgot the name of the film as soon as the title had left the screen. For some reason the names of its stars, Tony Curtis and Janet Leigh, lodged in his mind for days afterwards. He couldn't concentrate on the action and left after an hour. As he walked towards the exit he thought he heard someone say "that red haired bastard" from among the rows of seats.

A damp wind slapped him across the face as he stepped into the street. He wandered around the town in an intermittent drizzle, uncertain how to occupy himself and prey to doubts and dreads. He walked past the dark shops in the main street; a few strangers hurried by, their collars turned up against the weather. Turning a corner he glanced in the window of a cycle shop, with the vague notion that he should buy another bike - a new Raleigh tourer perhaps - so he could set off on a really long bicycle journey: to Scotland or the Lake District, anywhere, as long as it was far enough away. Far enough to get clear of his life... But he had nowhere near enough money, so he abandoned the idea and moved on.

As he came out of the end of a side street he caught sight of the massive blank outline of Reeds. The glimmer and flash of the furnaces seemed more vivid than usual, reflected from the low cloud that lay over the town. The air stank of sulphur. Christ, he thought, there are people in that place. He turned away quickly and retraced his steps up the street. He couldn't imagine himself in a steelworks. Reeds belonged to the life of another Ronald Patterson: someone who had never existed except in his father's head.

Passing the Espresso Coffee Bar he wondered if he should go in, or if the owner would remember him and tell him to get lost.

He pressed his face to the steamed up window to see who was inside and got a shock - the place was packed with teds from the estate. No sign of Ingo or Tiny and the rest. Maybe they had been thrown out by the teds, who seemed to have taken the place over. He couldn't see the ted with the tattoo - perhaps he was still recovering... As he peered through the window someone spotted him and pointed. An arm swung towards the glass and he stepped back as coffee dregs splattered over the inside of the window. He didn't want any more trouble and moved on quickly.

He sat on the seat by the war memorial and smoked a Du Maurier. Looking towards the river he could still see the furnaces at Reeds flickering on the low cloud. He turned in the other direction, towards the streets of terraced houses that ran, row after row, up the hill as far as St Margaret's church. He felt no affinity with the place. For the first time in his life he felt separate from the town, from its shabby streets and small-minded people. He didn't belong any more. He had no future there. But, then, he had no future anywhere.

By ten o'clock he was back home. His mother was in the dining room watching TV and he sat with her. Neither spoke. Some Saturday night series on ITV ended and a film began. He couldn't endure the strain of watching the emotional conflicts of other people's lives and went into the kitchen to make some toast. He was about to have a cup of tea when Big Red came in from the union club. His father was in his usual irritable mood and within a couple of minutes he was rowing with Nancy.

Young Red gulped his tea and fled upstairs to his room. He had bought himself a second-hand mains radio to keep the ghosts of the night at bay and to blot out his parents' arguments. He tuned in to Radio Luxembourg and wondered if Sally Bell was listening too. He tried to remember what she had told him about the different types of music, but all he could recall was her anger. He tuned the radio to a foreign music programme and Sally Bell's image slowly faded from his mind. Eventually he fell asleep.

Sunday was dry and sunny so he went for a bike ride with Chris. But an abyss had appeared between them and he couldn't talk. He was preoccupied with feelings of hopelessness and betrayal. Whenever Chris wanted to stop he insisted they kept going - he only felt safe when he was moving; when he was still it seemed that his anxieties were devouring his brain. After a few hours Chris became grumpy and said he wanted to go home. Young Red left him with a mere nod and cycled on. He didn't get back to the town until after dark.

On Monday Mouth didn't turn up for his paper round and neither he nor Sally Bell were at school. At mid-morning break Young Red sat in the Swamp on his own, smoking a Du Maurier and staring at the crumbling floodbank that hid the river. When he squeezed through the gap in the school fence at lunchtime he found Mouth waiting for him on the other side.

"Hey, old buddy," Mouth grinned. "Thought I'd just come to say adios."

"What? What d'you mean?" Young Red was gripped by a sense of foreboding.

"Mean I'm off - way out west. Into the sunset." Mouth's grin seemed as fixed as a mask. He turned and began walking towards the clump of willows.

"Let's have a cig and a sit down. A man needs to talk in private, away from this rubbish." He gestured at the school yard.

They located a couple of empty oil drums and sat behind the screen of summer leaves.

"Give us a cig, Red. It'll help me talk better."

Young Red passed him the Du Maurier.

"You didn't do your round this morning."

"Finished. That's all in the past. Best leave it there," Mouth's grin was back in place. "Going away. Hundred miles off."

"What?" Young Red tried to gather his shattered wits. "When?" "Tomorrer."

"But why? I mean... how long for?"

"For good, old buddy. For good," Mouth cleared his throat and spat at the remains of a rotting fruit box. "Leaving this shitty town. Going out west - to my uncle Harry's."

Young Red was dismayed, depressed, confused and disbelieving all at the same time. It was the first occasion he had heard Mouth mention an uncle Harry.

142

"But why? I mean - why so sudden?"

"My dad's got a new woman - a prize bitch! Curses me whenever I'm in. She's even going to the fights with him, 'stead of me! So I'm off!"

Mouth looked so sorrowful Young Red felt moved. He knew what it was like to be let down.

"Sorry, Mouth. It's a shame," he said feebly.

"Ain't it?" Mouth spat. His face was distorted with bitterness. "Ain't it just a bloody shame!" He glared at Young Red then looked down. "Should cut the bitch up and feed her to the fucking dogs!"

They were silent for a while, staring at the willows.

"What you going to do with your uncle?" Young Red wondered if he might be able to go too.

"Me and Harry'll be breeding horses. He's got a bit of land off a bloke he knows and we'll be keeping horses on it."

Young Red's hopes were destroyed. He didn't know anything about horses.

"But why horses for Chrissake? What d'you know about horses?"

"My dad's been round horses all his life. He's taught me all he knows."

Young Red felt that a stranger had appeared before him dressed in Mouth's memory. It was the first time in their friendship that he had ever mentioned horses. Who in this dump of a town knew anything about horses anyway? But, then, he reflected, Mouth and his dad must be two of the few who did. In fact, Young Red thought, Mouth could be a genius with horses as far as anyone knew - he had always kept so much of his life to himself.

"So I won't see you any more?" Young Red felt a lump in his throat.

"Doubt it." Mouth spat at the fruit box. "Say adios to Belly for me. She'll be glad I've gone." He laughed silently. "Thanks for the cig."

Young Red nodded. Mouth had never thanked him for anything ever before. Mouth stood up. His dark eyes scrutinised Young Red's dejected figure and seemed to probe his sadness.

"Cheer up! You got Belly all to yourself now! You've got all summer to take her to the priory - she'll be bow-legged as a jockey by September!" He patted Young Red on the shoulder. "And remember to keep her in cigs. That's your insurance!"

Young Red looked up at him and nodded, speechless.

Mouth left him alone in the willows, staring at the flickering leaves. It had been fun with Mouth. Good fun, but dangerous. But now, like Mouth had said, that was all in the past. Everything that had been any good was in the past. After a while, when the willow leaves became blurred, Young Red realised there were tears in his eyes.

When Young Red arrived at the paper shop on Tuesday morning Ralph was behind the counter, flapping about in his slippers and blowing like a walrus.

"Now then, Young Redskin. You get me them papers in and I'll sort them. Doing Len's round till I find a new lad."

Young Red opened the door and dragged the bundles in from the street.

"Would have offered it to you as well, but it'll take too long. Hope I ain't forgotten how to ride a bike!"

Ralph muttered and breathed heavily and sighed as he sorted the papers on the counter.

"Len didn't tell me he was leaving till yesterday. Wish he'd given me a bit of notice. Know anyone who might like a good round? Ten bob a week."

A pay rise - that would annoy Mouth if he knew, Young Red thought. It was only nine shillings last week. But all that was in the past.

"No, I don't. Better ask Dilly and Dally."

"Dilly and Dally, is it, Young Redskin?" Ralph chuckled and puffed behind the counter. "Len told me he's going out west. What the hell's that supposed to mean?"

"He's going to be one of the cowboys." Young Redskin replied without smiling.

So much for Mouth's insurance, Young Red thought, as he cycled off on his round. It was impossible to get any cigarettes with Ralph lurking everywhere at once. Anyway, he would be leaving the shop soon himself - and he was damned if he was going to spend his pay from Reeds on cigarettes for Sally Bell. She would have to look out for herself... But, if he stopped, would she tell her aunt he was a murderer?

It was as if he had conjured her up. As he cycled back through the town with his empty paper-bag he saw Sally Bell, in a smart long sleeved dress, crossing the street that led to the market square. It was only ten to eight - he checked his old Ingersoll to make sure. He couldn't believe she could get up so early, there was hardly a day when she hadn't been late for school.

"Hi, Red."

She waved when she saw him. He had to jam his heels down extra hard on the road so his brakeless bike could stop in time.

"Hi, Sal." He felt awkward. "You just got up or going to bed?"

"Cheeky sod! I'm off to work."

"Work?" Young Red's sense of reality deserted him completely. He felt numb.

"I did what you said. I've got a job at Nelson's, in their new record department! Started yesterday. Josie said they were looking for someone and I went on Saturday afternoon." Sally Bell looked down at the pavement. "I didn't want to at first... but then I thought, well - it's a chance... I had a chat with Mr Blake - the manager - and he asked me lots of questions - about what sort of music would be really a big thing in the sixties and stuff like that. And when I'd told him he said I was just right 'cos I could talk to everyone about the new releases."

Sally Bell was pleased with herself and smiled and giggled and couldn't stop talking. But her smiles had a privacy he wasn't meant to share. It was as if she was talking to her image in a mirror. She prattled on, "And they've put in new listening booths so's customers can hear stuff first afore they spend their money. And I can play what records I want, 'cos Mr Blake says it's a good way to bring people in. It's great! It's the best thing that ever happened!"

Young Red was hardly able to grasp what Sally Bell was saying. He tried to make a joke. "With a figure like that there won't be a bloke under thirty'll buy records anywhere but Nelson's!"

But making jokes wasn't what he wanted to do. He wanted to grab her and tell her let's go back to that day, long ago - that day in the sun with the swooping birds and the summer grass when we could touch and laugh and lie together as if nothing else mattered... Sally Bell smiled a private smile and tossed her heavy curls. It was as if she was pretending Saturday morning hadn't happened. But there was a frightening absence between them, a crack right through to the earth's core.

Young Red stared at the pavement. "Mouth's gone."

At the mention of Mouth her smile disappeared.

"Len? Where?"

"His uncle's. Hundred miles away. Says he's not coming back. Told me to say goodbye."

Young Red watched the waves of surprise and relief cross her face.

"Good... Good riddance to bad rubbish!"

"There's just you and me, now, Sal."

It wasn't what he wanted to say. What he wished to say was let's go back to where we began. What happened after was a bad dream. We've woken up now and it's over. Let's go back to being just me and you in the grass in the middle of the summer. But it was impossible - he couldn't even reach out and touch her sleeve.

"That's right, Red. Come and see me in the shop sometime if you like."

She smiled at him in her private triumph. The smile was an empty reflection from the past.

"I might just do that." Young Red felt his own hollow words drift away on the indifferent air.

"Have to go now, Red." She spoke brightly. "Got to help Mr Blake with the new display."

He watched her sexy walk until she turned the corner into the market square - the body that had been his to reach out and touch as often as he liked seemed to have flown away to the far side of the sun...

And now Sally Bell was at Nelson's she didn't need him at all. She could say what she wanted about him, to get her revenge on Mouth. She could say they had tormented her. She could tell what had happened at the river.

He noticed he was gripping the handlebars of his bike so hard his bloodless hands had gone completely white. Jesus, he thought. What friends can do to you. It was best not to have any ever.

Tuesday at school was an ordeal. Whenever he noticed Brock he was sniggering and saying something behind his hand to one of his new cronies. Young Red imagined he was whispering about him, saying what a thick ape he was and how useless he was at everything except shooting defenceless people.

At lunchtime he cycled into the town, with the idea of pleading with Sally Bell to forgive him. But when he rode past Nelson's he saw her coming out deep in conversation with a young man in a dark grey suit. Young Red felt hopelessly outclassed and rode away without her noticing him.

Somehow he got through the afternoon. When he arrived home his mother insisted he took Old Florrie a bag of groceries. He knocked on the front door of the old cottage at the top of the street and waited. After ages of knocking his grandmother appeared and gave him a sixpence in exchange for the groceries.

"Don't forget what I told you, lad," her strong voice grated at him from her tiny frame. "Cut your connections." She eyed him steadily from the doorway. "Get clear of your life and you'll get your life clear."

"Right, Gran. I'm working on it."

Half way down the street he turned and saw she was still watching him from her doorway. He waved at her and she stuck out her aged arm and waved back. He had an odd feeling as he rode on down the street. I'll never see her again, he thought. But he couldn't explain why.

He couldn't bear the thought of going home, so he cycled to the church on the top of the hill to escape the oppressive heat of the town. He sat on the churchyard wall in the shade of a tree. The air was cool and sweet under the tree and he was reluctant to plunge back into the stench and grime. He shifted his position on the wall and then wished he hadn't. In a gap between the bushes on the slope below the church he caught sight of the river, flashing in the sun like a warning. That river, he thought. The cause of all my problems.

On his way back into the town he caught up with Tommy Page the postman, cycling slowly with his fishing box on his back. He tried to get past before he was recognised, but it must have been his hair.

"Now then, young man, haven't seen you with your pikeing rod lately."

Tommy slowed to a stop, cutting in on Young Red, so he pulled up at the kerb behind him.

"No, Tommy, been too busy for fishing."

"Busy with the women, eh?"

Tommy cackled mischievously.

"I know what it's like!"

"No... not really... I... er... I've been doing a lot of biking."

Who the hell's been talking about me now, Young Red thought furiously.

"Got a grand catch last night."

Tommy half turned so he could see his audience. Young Red made no attempt to move closer.

"Never guess what it were."

Oh, shit, Young Red thought. Another of his fishermen's tales.

"No, Tommy. Mebbe a twenty pound pike!"

"Gerraway!" Tommy cackled good naturedly. "No - it weren't a fish I caught. I were down at the landing stages about this time of day and I hooked a bloody welly - a flaming wellington boot!"

It was like a dream. Young Red felt he was really fast asleep and dreaming. He couldn't say a word.

"I were fishing for livebait for pikeing by the landing stages - you know, downriver from the bridge in town."

Of course. Where else could they be? But it will be all right, Young Red thought, because I'll wake up soon. He managed a minimal nod.

"Well, I thought I'd got hooked on a snag - you know, bit of sunk tree come down in that flood..."

Tommy was relishing his tale. Young Red felt vacant, as if there was nothing supporting his head, just a billowing emptiness between his neck and his knees.

"Well..." Tommy continued, twisting around on his bike seat. "Thought I'd lost my line - you know - thought I'd have to cut it... But I said be patient, Tommy, lad, just you try and wind it in. No good losing hooks if you can help it. Hooks cost money. And - you know - whatever it were it were heavy for a light line, but it came. And I said well, Tommy, that ain't no snag..."

Young Red, to the left of Tommy's direct line of sight, kept his eyes fixed on the pavement.

"Well, I reeled it in and - you know - up come this welly... And it had a human leg in it!" Tommy's eyebrows shot up so high they almost vanished under his cap. Young Red felt as if he had been heavily drugged: his hands had gone dead and his face was growing numb. He couldn't speak.

Tommy, oblivious of Young Red's plight, continued at his leisurely fisherman's pace.

"Well, I told the bobbies and they came down and - you know - they took it away. Said they'd send it to the forensicals, or something. Well, I saw Mawson about ten minutes back and he said that leg belonged a lad of about twelve or thirteen and they'd be dragging the river tomorrer - you know - to see if they could find the rest of him. Said it were half eaten away with pike and that, but they reckoned - you know - that he'd been in the water a bit. Month or two mebbe. Clever fellers, them forensicals. Don't know how they do that sort of work though - looking at stuff like that every day. Worse than being a fellmonger! Now what d'you think of that?"

Vaguely Young Red realised Tommy was asking a question. But he couldn't respond. Tommy continued, under the spell of his own narration.

"Well, it gave me a fright - you know - finding that leg. I thought why did it have to be me? I'm a postman. Only for another three years and then I'll be done, but - you know - I'm a postman today. Why didn't them lads from the slaughterhouse find it? You know - they're used to bits of bodies and suchlike.

Or them rough youths from the bone mill, they're chopping them up all day..."

Tommy tried to catch Young Red's eye, but he got no reaction.

"Well, the bobbies said not to say nothing till - you know - till they had the report from the forensicals. Well, you're the first person I've seen since Mawson... I tell you, it were enough to put a man off his fishing, finding a thing like that!"

The instinct for survival came to Young Red's rescue.

"Shit, Tommy...' he mumbled. "Have to go for my tea!"

He escaped, cycling in a daze, his head thumping like a battle-zone, his limbs feeling weak and hollow as windsocks. Somehow he got home. His body must have known the way.

His body took him past the tea table, through the insect buzzing of his parents' protestations, up the stairs and into his room, where it flung him down on his bed, too ill to move. His mother came up and tapped on the door and, a while later, Janet asked from the landing if he wanted any tea. But he said he had a headache and they went away.

Eventually his mind began to work. The river must have risen and carried the boot as far as the little arc of mud near the bridge. Then the water must have gone down and left the boot behind. That must have been the moment when he saw it lying there. Then the river must have risen again that same day and lifted the boot off the mud. That was why he and Mouth couldn't find it. The river had carried the boot downstream, where it had got stuck in the weed near the landing stages and Tommy Page had hooked it. The river probably rose and fell several times a day during showery weather. Or - Young Red sat up in dismay as a fresh thought struck him - it could have been the second wellington boot... In that case what had happened to the first one?

He lay back and closed his eyes, feeling feverish. Images teemed through his head. He saw Mouth galloping bareback on a wide grassy plain, with mountains on one side and a view of the sea on the other. He saw Sally Bell lying on the floor in her record department, with the young man in the dark grey suit on top of her. He saw Brock playing cricket, wielding a huge bat, with Brock's father in his railway uniform at the other end of the wicket. Brock, white as a saviour, was hitting sixes, winning the match by himself, while his father applauded. No-one could stop him. Then he saw Raggy, with only one leg, crawling along a muddy riverbank. His face, like a long drowned sheep, was eaten completely away...

He buried his face in his pillow and tried to shut out the images. He was alone. Totally alone. There wasn't one person in this stupid town he could speak to ever again. Not one being he could confide in or ask for advice. Not one. Not ever. Anyway, they would arrest him soon and he would be gone.

Everything was happening too fast. Old Florrie had said something about having to be faster than light to see the truth. He couldn't see anything. He was too slow, like a stone. He lay for hours, his head in turmoil. Eventually it grew dark. He turned on his radio and the voices and music lulled him to sleep. Luxembourg finished at two in the morning and the silence woke him up. He slept again fitfully and dreamed...

He was running among a maze of ruined walls. At every turn he met Sally Bell who screamed that he had raped her. She pulled up her skirt and he saw the blood on her legs and he knew she had been a virgin. He punched her in the face and her head went rolling over the grass and he saw Mouth lunge at it with his knife. He could see policemen closing in on him and each one had Mawson's face. As he tried to hide from them he looked at his hands which were clutching packets of stolen cigarettes and he saw that the back of his hand was tattooed with the shape of a bird - a swallow in full flight.

Young Red left before six for the paper shop. He couldn't bear to be in the house. As he was cycling towards the market square a solitary youth in a boiler suit hailed him from the pavement. He stared at the figure without recognition.

"Thanks, Red." The figure gave him the thumbs-up. "I owe you one."

With a shock Young Red realised it was Ingo, on his way to the early shift at the bone mill. Ingo without his studs and sunglasses. On his own without his mates, without the best seat in the coffee bar. A figure in a worker's uniform, indistinguishable from a million others like him. The person he had risked his neck for, shuffling along like an old man to his daily drudgery... Young Red waved back and watched the anonymous figure until it turned a corner. Jesus, had Ingo always been like that?

He arrived at the paper shop and walked up and down in the alley till Ralph unlocked the door. He couldn't put his mind on the order of his round, so he bundled a handful of papers from each of the stacks into his bag and set off. Ralph was too busy pumping up the tyres on the shop bike to notice. Young Red shoved a few papers through the first letter boxes he came to and dumped the rest in a yard behind the cinema. He couldn't think what to do with them; he could no longer remember what they were for.

He cycled to the railway station cafe and bought a cup of tea and a bar of chocolate. He drank half the tea and ate a square of the chocolate but then felt sick and had to leave. He imagined every figure he saw in railway uniform was Brock's dad. By half past seven he was in the coke yard at the gas works, crouching behind a van, waiting for the men to go in for a tea-break. At eight o'clock they left the yard and filed into a grimy prefab.

Young Red covered the fifty yards between the van and the old shed in the corner in twenty strides. He knew the shed well - he'd climbed into it before for a dare. There was a ladder with several missing rungs that led to an open door about fifteen feet from the ground. He sprang at the ladder and was through the door in a moment. He stepped cautiously across the rotten floorboards to the window. Several panes were missing. From the empty square in the top left hand corner he had a perfect view of the course of the river through the town.

By nine o'clock the police had arrived at the bridge. There was a long flat-ended boat in the river; Young Red recognised it as the punt Old Shack used for cutting the riverweed when it had grown too thick and threatened to block the channel. The Shackletons, father and son, were in the boat; he knew it was Young Shack from his mass of hair. Policemen were coming down

152

the bank with poles and the sunlight kept flashing on something in Young Shack's hands. They didn't seem to have any nets, but they were too far away for Young Red to be sure. The inboard motor on the boat started up and boat and policemen moved slowly upriver.

The operation began below the bone mill siding and worked upriver from there. Young Red could see, almost a mile upstream, a group of figures assembled in the field below the Roman Camp. A dinghy was pushed out from the bank with three figures aboard dressed in black. Two of the figures rolled backwards into the water and disappeared. Young Red, mesmerised by the scene on the river and too horrified to move, stared from the window, oblivious of the men working below him in the yard.

By early afternoon the boats were less than two hundred yards apart. The divers had been gone from the dinghy a long time and when they resurfaced one of them waved his arms. The police on the bank stopped probing and Young Shack stood up in the punt. Young Red could clearly hear shouting and then a commotion began in the yard below him. Some of the gas works men were watching from the wall and Young Red could hear their voices. But he didn't need a commentary, because he knew, before the dark thing was heaved into the punt, that the divers had found Raggy's body.

Chapter Fourteen

Young Red escaped from the gas works when the men went into the prefab at the two o'clock shift change. The commotion on the river was over; the punt and the dinghy had disappeared downstream. Cycling back towards the bridge to his side of town he had to wait while a policeman held up the traffic. Trapped between a truck and a Ford Popular he approached the bridge at little more than walking pace. He had a good view: the Shackletons and two policemen were heaving a stretcher into the back of a police van parked on the bridge. On the stretcher was a thing under a cover. A lump. Water was dripping from the stretcher and a length of riverweed trailed on to the road. A policeman pulled at the trailing weed and disturbed the edge of the cover. Young Red, as he crept slowly past, caught a glimpse of something dark and wet underneath.

It was because of him. Everything that had happened on the river today was because of him. The police, the water bailiff, the boats, the crowds at the bridge watching... Then it would be in the papers and that would be because of him too. The pictures, the shrieking headlines. Because of him.

It was because of him that they had put something into the back of a police van. Something dark and wet, with a piece of trailing weed. A lump. A thing under a cover. A silent thing in the back of a van... A gaping crowd at the end of a bridge... The blackest of headlines...

Because of him.

But it had been such a simple thing. Running through the flooded riverside fields playing a game. A chase. A simple thing. Splashing through the water with your pals. Shouting. Laughing. Having fun... Why not have fun? When you got older the fun stopped - so why not? Going down the river. Shooting coot. Hunting. Pulling a trigger. A simple, harmless thing...

Young Red wheeled the Carlton along the deserted lane, trying to control himself, trying to collect his thoughts. The lane led to an abandoned quarry where he would be safe. Safe for a few hours while he decided what to do. While he made a plan. While he worked out his side of the story.

But he didn't have a story; didn't have a side. When the truth came out it would be faster than the speed of light. Sally Bell would tell. Brock would tell. They would say he was mad. They would say his grandmother was a witch. They would say that he was a murderer. Then Mawson would arrest him and they would take him away in handcuffs and the man in the suit behind the desk would say he understood and get him to sign a confession and give him a cup of tea.

He wandered about in the quarry obsessed by thoughts of death. Would

they hang him like they had that young bloke in London? He could remember his parents talking about it years ago. And he hadn't even done the shooting... Would they put him in a mental asylum? What was it like in a padded cell? Would he be able to go to the toilet in a straitjacket?

Young Red wandered through the deserted buildings. Could he live here, perhaps? But what would he eat? Could he catch rabbits and hares like Shack? But what would he catch them with? He didn't want anything to do with guns ever again.

He came to a large shed with walls of rusty corrugated iron. Some of the sheets of iron were loose and creaked and screeched in the wind with metallic voices. In the shed was a large steel beam with a thick rope hanging from it. Young Red could just reach the end of the rope if he stood on his toes. The sight of the rope gave him another idea: should he hang himself and spare himself the misery of trial and imprisonment? He pictured himself hanging from the beam, swaying in the gusts of wind that came in through the gaps in the walls, with the metallic grating of the rusty shed all around him. He left the shed quickly and stepped out into the sunlight.

But why shouldn't he live? Why shouldn't he come and go as he wanted? It had been an accident, after all. It wasn't fair that he should die because of an accident. But he had no friends, no-one who would speak up for him. He didn't have a story. He didn't have a side.

The sun was setting and the shadows on the cricket field were long and sombre. Young Red hid his bike among the weeds by the hedge and skulked behind the pavilion listening. The pavilion was in darkness, but he could hear voices from somewhere. He edged around to the side of the pavilion steps and he saw them: two figures in the nets, one bowling, one batting. Two bikes against the pavilion railings. Two voices, slightly raw and unfinished: two teenagers...

"Just one more over, Andy, and then we're off. Promise."

"You said that two overs ago."

"Just one more. Got to get this stroke right afore Sunday."

"That's it. That's the last ball. Can't see what I'm doing. We'll have to come back tomorrer."

"Shit! I was just getting it right!"

A figure approached the pavilion and leapt astride one of the bikes.

"Got to go! See you tomorrer."

"Okay, Andy. I'm coming. I'll catch you up."

As the first youth rode away into the gloom Young Red stepped out from the side of the pavilion. He had a heavy iron bar in his hand that he had brought from the quarry. He strolled towards the practice net. The second figure was at the far end, tapping a stump into the ground with the end of his bat handle.

"Now then, Brockless, you prickless freak. It's my turn to do a spot of batting."

Brock turned in surprise.

"Red! What you doing here?" There was a husky edge of fear in his voice, but he overcame it with sarcasm. "Run out of folks to shoot?"

"I ain't come to play games, Brockless. Games is for kids." Young Red kept his voice as steady and hard as he could.

"Run out of friends, have you? Going crazy 'cos they found something in the river?" Keeping his eyes on Young Red Brock moved away from the stumps and gripped his bat with both hands.

"It's you what's run out of friends, Brockless. Ain't no-one to help you here."

156

Young Red withdrew the iron bar from behind his back. Brock faced him along the length of the practice net. "Why don't you own up? Why don't you tell them? Mebbe they'll feel sorry for you 'cos you're too thick to know what you're doing!"

"Shut your face, you little shit!" Young Red took several menacing steps down the pitch. "If you don't, I'll shut it with this!"

He raised the iron bar as high as his ear. Brock took a step backwards and lifted the bat in front of his chest.

"My dad's coming down in a minute. He finds you here he'll slaughter you!" The edge of fear had returned.

"Lying bastard!" Young Red stepped closer. "Don't care if he comes - I'll smash him to bits with this!" He waved the iron bar in front of his face.

"Won't do you no good killing me." Brock backed behind the stumps. "I've wrote it all down on a piece of paper in my bedroom. How you shot Raggy and laughed as he floated away! How you were bragging you'd shoot anyone who told! How you shot that lad from the estate and tried to knife his brother in the coffee bar! How you and Mouth been stealing cigs for months from Ralph's and giving them to Belly so you can screw her down the priory!"

Young Red roared with fury, but Brock was too quick for him. He pulled out one of the stumps and flung it at Young Red's head. The stump caught Young Red a glancing blow on the temple and Brock was past him before he could regain his wits. Brock was running for his bike. Young Red cut him off. Brock changed direction and rushed up the steps of the pavilion. Young Red caught him at the top and they fell together through the double doors, smashing the lock and shattering the long glass panes. They crashed on to the floor and rolled apart. Young Red scrambled to his feet and shook himself like a dog. He had lost the iron bar, but he grabbed a wooden chair instead and raised it in the air above Brock's body.

The figure on the floor didn't move. Its stillness cut through Young Red's rage like a lightning flash. He lowered the chair and flung it away from him. Kneeling, he peered at the form on the floor. Was there blood? Was Brock dead?

Before Young Red could react Brock's foot shot into his stomach. With a cry of pain and fury he doubled up as Brock got to his feet preparing to flee. Young Red was up too in a second and his flying tackle brought them both down again in a mass of broken chairs and overturned tables. They got to their feet at the same time, Brock backing away, Young Red advancing. A blow to the middle of the forehead sent Brock down again. He struggled on to his elbows and knees, moaning. Young Red waited for him to get up - he wanted to see the fear in his tormentor's face, wanted to hear him blubber and plead. He felt purposeful and dangerous, without a shred of pity in his being. As he watched Brock's struggles he caught a glimpse through a window of lights moving outside.

A car was turning off the road into the entrance of the cricket field. For a moment Young Red hovered above his victim, uncertain what to do. Then, with a curse, he sprang down the pavilion steps and sprinted to the hedge for his bike. Seconds later he was over the fence at the far end of the field and cycling away into the darkness.

A three-quarter moon sped through tufts of cloud. The riverside fields were silent, washed with flying light and shadow. Young Red stood on the riverbank above one of the deepest places he knew and looked down at the Carlton. He was sweating; it had been a long haul in the dark from the Roman Camp. The moon disappeared behind a cloud as the bike hit the water. He heard the splash but, when the moon reappeared, there was no sign the bike had ever existed. Turning away from the river, Young Red plodded across the field.

He walked for a long time through the fields, occasionally stumbling when the moon was obscured by cloud and he was plunged into darkness. He tried to aim for the field gates, as they had on the day of the flood, in case he fell into a ditch. In the moonlight he could pick out the gaps in the hedgelines where the gates came but, when the moon went in, he lost his bearings and wandered around like a drunk until the moon came out again. He couldn't stop walking. The idea of sitting on the grass to wait for the moon to come back was intolerable.

As he was about to climb over a gate he heard a rifle shot. Then another. In panic he ducked down by the gatepost. Was it Upshot Bagley? Surely not. The shooting tenant wouldn't be out this late and, anyway, he would be using a shotgun... Another shot. Almost simultaneously a bullet smacked into the gatepost a yard from where he crouched. Oh, shit! They were after him! Now it was his turn to run while people chased him over the fields with guns! His heart raced; these were real bullets, not air-rifle slugs... Which way should he go? Should he run to Wild Man and hide among the trees? He'd have to try, or he was dead. But the wood was several fields away...

"Come out of there with your hands wide, or the next one goes through your neck!"

Shack! he thought.

"Shack - don't shoot! It's me! It's Red! Don't shoot! Don't shoot!"

He saw a figure approaching down the hedgeside, watching him along the barrel of a rifle. He stood up.

"Oh, Shack. I've got problems. I've got to get away."

The rifle was lowered. Young Shack was at the gate.

"Best come back with me, Young Red, and have a bite to eat."

They walked in silence to a little copse a couple of fields away. Shack poked an air-hole in the small fire he had covered with leaves and threw on a handful of twigs. Young Red crouched close to the flames, feeling exhausted and ill.

"I was... I was just walking about down here, trying to think what to do."

Young Red decided to tell Shack as little as possible. He chewed on a piece of cold rabbit meat, hoping his desperation wouldn't show.

"Going to Reeds ain't for me. It ain't the life I want."

"I can understand that." Shack was expertly skinning one of the rabbits he had shot, working almost without looking, as if his hands had eyes. "I can understand the need to get free of all that."

He set the rabbit over the fire to cook and began trimming short sticks for snare stakes with his big sheath-knife.

"Bad business on the river today."

Young Red's nerves jumped as if he had touched a live electric circuit. How much did Shack know? How much did he remember from the day of the flood?

"Don't know anything about it, Shack. Been busy at school today."

"Found that young lad. That Richard Bottomley. Him what went missing a bit back."

Shack went on trimming stakes. Young Red couldn't tell if he was watching him or not, Shack's face was hidden in fire-shadow.

"I'd forgot all about him, Shack. You forget folks when they're not around."

"Must have been there all along. Found him up a big storm drain everyone had forgot were there. All fast with weed and trapped by a great tree root. Been there for evermore if that diver hadn't thought to look in. Just turn that meat a bit, will you?"

Young Red turned the rabbit over the fire.

"How'd he got in the drain? Be full of water pouring out, wouldn't it?"

"Must be blocked under the town some place."

Shack scrutinised the ends of his sharpened stakes, holding them up against the moon.

"Only water what was in it were coming in from the river. Diver said it were like a great black cave in that drain, but he went in, 'cos he had a feeling there was something in there."

Young Red didn't want to talk about Raggy - he didn't want Shack to start making connections - so he tried to change the subject.

"Len Dykes has left town. Didn't get on with his dad's new woman, so he's gone to work with horses."

Shack fastened the sharpened stakes together and tossed the bundle aside.

"That's all you can do if it don't suit you where you are. If you stay you get poisoned. You get like a pond: just lying there catching all the shit other people chuck in. Till you get bitter and

160

nothing can drink there. Then you get foul and everything hates being near you. Best leave. Keep clean. Keep flowing like fast water."

When the rabbit was cooked they ate a little of it, Young Red juggling the hot meat in his hands. It reminded him of the day of the flood, when Raggy had eaten meat with Shack too. But whatever Shack knew, or suspected, he wasn't saying anything. He wasn't asking questions. Perhaps, Young Red hoped, Shack had simply forgotten.

"Going to set a few snares down a couple of hedgesides while there's still a bit of moonlight."

Shack stood up.

"Have what meat you want - and take a bit with you when you go. Be a long day for you tomorrer." He paused. Young Red nodded his thanks, looking up at him apprehensively.

"A long day, Shack?"

"There's a Polish fella camped up on the top road. He'll be going north tomorrer. Got a big contract up in the forestry. Planting and thinning and such. He were talking to my dad yesterday. Told him he's looking for strong lads who don't mind living rough. Long term, he said. Plenty of work. Good money. Goes all over England. Scotland as well, he said. Been here afore, recruiting, like. He told my dad he'd be leaving tomorrer. Best be there at first light. Brown truck with a Douglas Fir painted on the door."

Shack vanished from the circle of firelight, leaving Young Red lying on the earth in his windcheater. He drifted into exhausted sleep, warmed by the hot meat and the fire...

He woke up once with a start. Shack was still not around, so he put more sticks on the fire. As he stared at the flames the image of Brock kneeling on the pavilion floor filled his head. Whether I stay or leave, he thought, Brock will do his worst. He'll accuse me of attacking him. He'll accuse me of murder. Then they'll look at Raggy's body... And then I'll go to gaol.

Young Red watched the last veils of mist lifting away from the land as the sun rose above the distant skyline. He had never viewed the whole valley at this hour of the day before; he had only ever seen the few deserted streets he had cycled through on his way to the paper shop. He had never realised how small the town was, surrounded by the immense empty skylines. It seemed such a tiny place to have had such big problems. He could hardly believe you could have any problems at all in a river valley at sunrise.

There was no room for him with the three older men in the cab, so he sat on the back of the truck with the gear, watching the swaying caravan that was hitched up behind. He was glad there were only the four of them; no-one else from the town had turned up, so the Pole had been keen to take him. Stay-at-homes, the lot, Young Red thought, stuck in that stupid little town like pigs in a bog, with their stupid little jobs and their stupid little houses. His roof was the sky, like Young Shack; his house was the whole world. I'll be a real wild man one day, he thought. Just like Shack.

As the sun climbed higher he caught a glimpse of the priory, its pale
stone reflecting the light, and the river, flashing like liquid silver. He could see St Margaret's church on the hill, its spire black against the sky and the field to the east that must be the Roman Camp. Then the truck turned a corner and ran between trees and the entire vision vanished like a dream.

He was moving; he was out on the open road and moving. Nothing could touch him now. Nothing could get to him. As long as he was moving he would be all right. And it was better than cycling. On the back of the truck it was almost as fast as flying...

Hour after hour the truck chugged north. The landscapes changed. Towns came and went, fields and villages and rivers arrived and departed. They stopped for a break around mid-morning and the Pole gave him a thick wedge of brown bread and a drink of black tea from his flask.

"What you say your name?" The Pole asked Young Red as they drank.

"Bob." Young Red replied, keeping his eyes on the Pole's face.

"Bob." The Pole said the name several times, as if trying to be sure his mouth would be happy with the sound of the name inside it. "Bob... Bob..."

He smiled at Young Red. "Is dog's name, Bob?"

Young Red smiled back. "Short for Robert."

"Ah, Robert. Yes... I call you Bob." The Pole decided. "Here, Bob. There, Bob. Good boy, Bob."

He laughed. Bob laughed too.

"My name Stefan. Is a good name."

They moved on. The sun reached the zenith and headed west. Way out west, into the sunset, Young Red thought. Shrewsbury today, Newcastle tomorrow, as someone had once said to him. That was fine by him. Fine. He had cut his connections. He had got clear of his life. And you couldn't do better than that.

CHAPTER FIFTEEN

Bob leaned on the churchyard wall, staring across the fields towards the river. That must be the place where he had got rid of the Carlton. Hard to remember that sort of detail, it was so long ago. There had been a hedge on the right, he was sure... It could have been that one - or maybe the one over there... The riverside fields looked different from the way he had remembered them; rank grass, broken fences, scrawny hedgesides - not as picturesque as he had thought at all.

That small clump of trees would have been the spot where he ate his last meal with Shack... And there, across those few fields, was the wood called Wild Man, where all the trouble had started... Further inland were the pale stones of the priory - at the sight of them the image of Sally Bell reappeared in his mind. "Red," she had said, "Red, will you look after me one day, if no-one else'll have me - when I get old like Connie Potter?" And his reply, "Course, Sal. Just give me a shout."

She hadn't shouted. But, then, she wouldn't have wanted to. The last time he had seen her she had been at the beginning of a new life. At least he had helped her get started... And anyway, if he had ever crossed her mind, he would have been hundreds of miles beyond her reach... He still thought of her now and then - as she was on that summer day in the sun-filled cloister, with her aunt's tight skirt and broken shoe. He thought of her too much.

Bob sighed. He had fled from the disaster of his life, from a world he had outgrown, but he had carried its ghosts with him; he had fled with his feet set in concrete - dragging a small town in a river valley behind him, with its burden of fear and betrayal.

He had gone north with Stefan and entered a world which had, as it turned out, a longer lifespan than steel. Bob smiled. So much for progress... He had spent his life among trees and had planted new generations which would not be due for felling until he was sixty-five. Now that was the best kind of insurance.

The work had changed him. In the forests he had grown close

to the rhythm of life - and closer to death too... He had taken over Stefan's business when the old Pole died - but, in spite of this modest success, he had failed, after all, to cut his connections. The loyal tormentors of the past had never abandoned him.

You had to accept there are things that can never be forgotten. You can forgive the ghosts of the past, even when they eat at your table and wake you in the night because they can't sleep. But you can never forget them. Never cut your connections entirely. Old Florrie must have known that - she wasn't inhuman.

Bob began to wish he hadn't stopped. There were too many ghosts in these fields - too many riverside shades of Young Red. Coming back had reopened wounds that no remedy on earth could ever completely heal.

He hadn't become a wild man. He'd become a boss. But a boss who spent most of his working hours out in the woods. Better than being trapped in the hell of a steel mill... They'd have to bury him in one of those forests - up in the Grampians or in Wales or North Yorkshire... He had no other home.

He loved those forests: their silence and otherness. When he was in them he often had the sense of his own insignificance - the feeling that had beset him on the riverbank and at Wild Man - but the difference was that now he saw himself, his species, as intruders. It would have been better if we had stayed with the monkeys, he thought, than to have become clever without being wise. Better for such dangerous tribes to have stayed swinging happily through the branches...

They were clear felling mostly in the forests these days and burning the brash. His tea always tasted of woodsmoke. Sometimes one of the loggers would shoot a rabbit and he would skin it and cook it for them over a small fire of twigs. At such times he would think of that meal in Shack's camp at Wild Man: the four of them there, listening to the tale of the old farmer who became one with the woods... But he never said a word to the lads; never spoke of his past to anyone. He would just sit feeding the fire from the stack of dry twigs, turning the meat, letting his hands work as if they had eyes of their own, while he was in another time and place: seeing Mouth lunge for the sheath-knife, hearing Shack's cautionary rebuke... Tea just wasn't the same brewed indoors. Its natural flavour was woodsmoke.

He still had the scar on his left cheek, and ran his fingers over it when he was upset, when the past came at him unexpectedly. He was doing it now, thinking of Sally Bell, as he stared at the sunlit stones of the priory. But if he and Sally Bell ever met again would they even recognise each other? Probably not. And they would surely be horrified at the ravages of the years. Best to remember her as she was: a strange, sad, beautiful girl, that no-one else but he had made love to.

He could have come back. He had thought often that the authorities would have been happy to wrap up Raggy's death with a verdict of misadventure. Whatever George Brockless had said. That red mark on Raggy's forehead could have been from a submerged root, or a fence-stake - it was hardly likely to have been the result of an airgun slug... But, because of the accusation, he would have been a pariah: he had shot at a boy and, directly or indirectly, had caused his death. How could you live among folks who knew a thing like that? It was true: staying or leaving, either way, his life had been damned.

No - he could never have come back. He should never have come back. He had tried to reconnect Young Red and Robert Patten, so they might treat each other with a little more sympathy. Well, would they? Had he achieved anything? Perhaps... Perhaps. The last word on a life.

The clock in St Margaret's church tower shook him as it struck the hour. Seven o'clock. Time to go. To head north. The lads would be waiting for him at Scotch Corner. There was no point staying longer; no point looking up the dead - or the living dead. No point reopening more wounds. As Mouth had once said that was all in the past. Best leave it there.

Bob smiled to himself as he shut the churchyard gate. Sure, Mouth. Sure. If you can.

Other New Titles from Springboard

If you have enjoyed this book why not get another good read from our fiction imprint Springboard? You can order our books in any bookshop or write direct to Yorkshire Art Circus, FREEPOST LS2336, Castleford WF10 4BR. Please make cheques payable to Yorkshire Art Circus Ltd. If you prefer to use an Access or Visa credit card please ring 01977 603028 and we will take your order immediately. Please quote order reference FL/95.

Postage and packing free (UK only). Please allow 28 days for delivery.

The Labour Man
Jim Wilson

Harry Beamish, lifelong socialist, wrenches a marginal seat from the Tories in an election which returns a Labour Government with a majority of one. The future of the Government and socialism depends on Harry.

Unfortunate, then, that he's done a bunk.

Harry's desperate attempts to rediscover his ideals reflect a wider crisis — "Can there be honour in politics?"

Jim Wilson's wicked look at power in the 90s will have you laughing all the way to the polls.

Price: **£4.99**   ISBN 1 898311 01 3